Walton
THE K9 FILES

Dale Mayer

WALTON: THE K9 FILES, BOOK 26
Beverly Dale Mayer
Valley Publishing Ltd.

Copyright © 2024

This is a work of fiction. Names, characters, places, brands, media, and incidents are either the product of the author's imagination or are used fictitiously. Any resemblance to actual events, locales, or persons, living or dead, is entirely coincidental.

ISBN-13: 978-1-778863-78-3
Print Edition

Books in This Series:

Ethan, Book 1

Pierce, Book 2

Zane, Book 3

Blaze, Book 4

Lucas, Book 5

Parker, Book 6

Carter, Book 7

Weston, Book 8

Greyson, Book 9

Rowan, Book 10

Caleb, Book 11

Kurt, Book 12

Tucker, Book 13

Harley, Book 14

Kyron, Book 15

Jenner, Book 16

Rhys, Book 17

Landon, Book 18

Harper, Book 19

Kascius, Book 20

Declan, Book 21

Bauer, Book 22

Delta, Book 23

Conall, Book 24

Baron, Book 25

Walton, Book 26

Cage, Book 27

Boxed Sets and Bundles

https://geni.us/Bundlepage

About This Book

Welcome to the all new K9 Files series reconnecting readers with the unforgettable men from SEALs of Steel in a new series of action packed, page turning romantic suspense that fans have come to expect from USA TODAY Bestselling author Dale Mayer. Pssst… you'll meet other favorite characters from SEALs of Honor and Heroes for Hire too!

Walton Headly enjoys getting out and being as active as he can be, given his missing leg. However, playing soccer now is hard to adapt to, compared to playing soccer before his injury. He has been in rehab for a long time and now reaches a need to do more. Searching for a missing War Dog sounds like a great way to ease back into a working life.

Chelsea Brown, a physical therapist, had helped get Walton back on his feet. He is one hell of a man but is struggling after that last soccer game. Her invitation to contact her older brother at his hunting lodge for any information on the missing War Dog yields more than expected. Together they head north to visit her brother and to check out the dog, who has just arrived with the new guests.

Finding out the guests are not ordinary hunters—and the dog is not an ordinary dog—causes conflict from the first meet. And goes steadily downhill. When the dog's owner turns up dead, all hell breaks loose. It's all Walton can do to keep the two—no make that three—of them safe …

Sign up to be notified of all Dale's releases here!
https://geni.us/DaleNews

K AT FROWNED AT Badger. "Are you telling me that Baron was working undercover the whole time?"

He nodded.

"That sneaky little bastard."

"I assumed you knew that. When you mentioned his name, I knew it was in some document in that file of yours," he noted, "and I had to make a few phone calls to figure out what was going on. It's one of the reasons I kept tabs on Baron a little closer."

"And he solved his undercover case too, as well as finding Kingston," she said. "That's amazing."

"Isn't it? I know I'm really happy with it."

"So you should be," she stated. "This is huge."

"And now what?" he asked.

"I have only one more file on the table, one more right now, but I'm not sure it'll be the end though."

"Maybe not," Badger agreed, "but we'll take it one at a time. Tell me about this one."

"Believe it or not, it's back to Alaska again."

He stared at her and shook his head. "How much will the flight cost?"

"I had to get a little cagey to cut that down, so I have a client already in Alaska, who would be a good fit."

He stared at her, his eyebrow shooting up. "My God, are

you so well-known now that we have people everywhere?"

"Maybe," she quipped, with a smile. "I haven't talked to him about it and don't know if it's something he's interested in, but he was a K9 trainer in the military for quite a few years. He lost several of his best friends in the process and ended up injured in an accident not long afterward. So maybe, just maybe …"

"And what's his name?"

"Walton."

Badger's eyebrow shot up again. "You do understand that I know him, right?"

"Of course," she replied. "You know everybody. Maybe not everybody, but you do know a lot of people. And it makes sense that you would know this one. … Plus, we still have Timber to deal with."

Badger's frown was immediate.

She nodded. "I know," she said, "but he's heading into his own place. We need to give him as much help as we can."

"I don't have a problem with that, but …" His voice trailed off, as he stared into the distance, but he finally nodded. "I know that Timber's time is coming, but I also know that a big mystery is in the back of his world too. Maybe we need to help him with that."

"As soon as he gets set up and settled."

"I'm not sure he's quite ready for that, so let's figure it out as we go."

She added, "I want to help him too."

"You do know that you can't help everyone, right?"

"I know that," she said, rolling her eyes as she got up. Then she neared Badger and looped her arms around him, giving him a big hug. "But I still want to try to help everyone who crosses my path." She kissed him on the cheek and turned to walk away.

He watched the woman of his life, the woman of his heart, and realized again just how damn special she was. She stopped at the doorway, smiled back at him, and added, "Besides, I have a really big heart and room for a lot more, … lots and lots more."

CHAPTER 1

WALTON HEADLY RETURNED his phone to his pocket and turned to the teammates he was sharing a beer with. It was a late Sunday afternoon, and they had been playing a friendly game of soccer for the last few hours, now relaxing and chilling over a couple cold ones. Most of the guys would get up and leave soon, and Walton knew he probably should too, particularly after that call.

Tony started to laugh. "What's the matter, dude? You look as if you just lost your best friend."

Walton shook his head and replied, "No, not at all. ... Nothing like that."

"Whatever it is seems to have you confounded."

He shrugged. "Have you guys ever heard about somebody up here adopting a War Dog?"

They frowned at him. Johnny pointed out, "Nobody would call it a War Dog, would they? Wouldn't it just be a dog?"

"Maybe," Tony added, "unless whoever it is wanted the cachet of having a War Dog, and we know lots of people around here who probably would."

Walton shrugged. "I suppose that's possible too."

Tony faced Walton. "Why? What difference does it make?"

"You guys know Kat?" Walton asked.

"We know that *you* know Kat," Tony joked. "She's the one who built you a leg that has you out here playing soccer with us."

"Too bad she didn't give you any skills to go with it," Johnny noted in his typical teasing tone.

Walton took the ribbing in a good-natured manner because that's just what it was. The fact was, Walton was damn glad to have what mobility he did. And, if a prosthetic allowed him to get out and to play soccer, he was all for it. Did he miss the ball sometimes? Yeah. Did the guys laugh even louder and cheer him on when he made a solid kick? Yeah. They all knew what he was up against, and they didn't have an ax to grind about it, which made life here a whole lot easier.

Walton explained, "She called me, and apparently they have been asked to look into multiple military dogs that were retired and adopted out. Their wellness check in this particular case couldn't locate the owner or the War Dog."

"Up here, they've probably gone hunting. Maybe they headed to one of their old hunting grounds, and they're just not in radio contact right now."

Walton nodded. "That's what I told Kat, and she just asked if I could check it out, if I had the time to spare."

Johnny laughed. "Spare time? Dude, you've got nothing but spare time. It's not as if you're out there carving and making a life for yourself or anything."

Again with the laughter and the jokes, but Walton just smiled because these guys were really supportive of his making a career as a carver. He'd been carving for a very long time, but he really never had the time, energy, or space to make a go of it, not until after his accident. Even then the *accident* wasn't something he took kindly to. It wasn't as if he was thrilled to have time on his hands, so he could stay home and carve. It was a goddamn disaster and definitely not what he'd signed up for.

But then nobody ever signed up for accidents, and still they happened, so who was he to blame anybody for it? "Shut the hell up," Walton grumbled.

"Touchy much? We're just saying that you can take some time, make a few inquiries around town," Johnny suggested. "If they've renamed the War Dog, no way you'll know for sure."

"Maybe."

"Actually," Brian offered, raising his hand, "check with the local vet clinics."

"Yeah, and how many are there around here?"

Brian tilted his head. "Don't know, but a lot, I would think."

"Did she say *where* in Alaska?" Johnny asked. "Because everybody seems to think we're just some small chunk of frozen pond, but knowing the space as we do, it's huge and an awful lot of ground to cover."

"She knows. Kat's sending me the information she has. She wanted to know if I was up for the job first."

"Any money come with it?" Johnny asked, with a waggle of his eyebrows. "Money is always good."

Walton chuckled. "Sorry, in this case, no money. It's strictly a volunteer gig."

"Yeah, but, if it puts you in good standing with the person who looks after your prosthetic, that's got to be worth something. Maybe a favor now will help with a favor later."

"Maybe so," Walton conceded, "but I wouldn't do it for that reason. I did plenty of K9 training when I was overseas. So, if I can help one of those animals now, I won't say no."

Several of the men rolled their eyes.

Nobody else in this group had been in the military. Yet, just because they hadn't, they were all standing here on their own two legs, whereas Walton was standing on a prosthetic. Such was his life. He looked down at his left hand, which was missing two fingers. If that was the price he paid in service to his country, he was good with it. So far, he'd managed with just three fingers on that hand. Yet it was amazing how much those two missing fingers altered his day-to-day life. Not to mention his missing leg.

"Dude, you came back in pieces. Haven't you given up enough of your life for that?" Brian spoke in a tone harsher than Walton expected.

"Maybe," he said, turning to look at the man, "but I did what I needed to do at the time."

Barry shook his head and finally spoke up. "But you of all people, ... Christ. You were the best soccer player out here before."

Walton winced at that *before* reference, meaning that he sucked at soccer now. "I know I'm holding you back," he stated, trying not to sound as stiff and as pissed off as he felt.

Immediately Barry jumped on that. "Look. We're just playing for fun, so it's not a big deal. Forget I said anything."

"But just so we all know and are all clear on this, we're still talking about setting up an actual team," Brian declared, "in which case, Walton won't play."

Stan, who had stayed out of this whole conversation, sent a warning glare to Brian.

"Maybe not," Walton agreed, with a shrug, "and maybe I don't care to anyway." With that, he stood up. "Time for me to go find a War Dog."

With a wave to the guys, he turned and strolled off, trying to make his exit a little more elegant than his arrival pregame. His stump had been pretty damn sore when he'd arrived, limping in, so Kat would admonish him about playing in the soccer game. But, damn, it was one of the things he'd always loved and still did. Yet the stump pain was a constant part of it now.

These guys were right. Walton hated admitting it, but they were. Walton had been a good soccer player, as in damn good. But then he'd chosen the military, and with that came all kinds of things he hadn't expected. His buddies obviously still held a few things against him.

As Walton walked away, he heard the others chiding Brian, their comments floating toward Walton, even as they tried to keep their voices down.

"Jesus, you didn't have to say that," Stan told Brian. "Walton's doing the best he can, and it's not hurting a thing. The game is a game, just for fun."

"Yeah, it's for fun right now," Brian clarified, "but we were doing this in order to set up a competitive team. I get that he's here and that he can do what he can do, but you know damn well he can't play in a league."

Walton wasn't so sure about that. If a few more adjustments were made to give him better balance, he could play better. They all thought it was pretty funny when he wiped out after the first couple kicks, though initially it had resulted in concern. Now when he fell, the comments were more routine, such as, *And down he goes, … timber!*

It had become a standing joke, and Walton appreciated that because it was a whole lot easier than any pity. The last thing he wanted was anybody racing to pick him up again. If he fell, he would damn well get back up on his own two legs.

He walked slowly to his truck, a little less defiantly now,

when a woman approached him.

"Are you okay?" she asked softly.

He stiffened and looked back at his physiotherapist. "Any reason I wouldn't be?" he asked, his tone cool.

She didn't say anything at first but studied him closely. "You tell me. I saw what happened when you came out that door. All of a sudden … you gave up the pretense."

"Some days you have to put on a little show—more than others."

Her lips twisted. "Are they hassling you again?"

"No, they aren't," he replied curtly. "We had a long game of soccer, and it was fun."

"Until it wasn't fun anymore," she pointed out.

"*I* thought it was fun," he clarified, "but I guess they're working toward a soccer league team here locally, and some feel I'm holding them back."

"No, you're not," she stated. "I drove by you guys today and stopped because you were doing a hell of a job."

He shook his head. "*Right*. What did I do? Fall twice?"

"Yes, only twice," she pointed out. "How many times have you fallen in the last few games?"

He turned to her and shook his head. "Always the cheerleader."

"Sometimes you need a cheerleader, and sometimes you just need to be yourself." And, with that, she turned and walked away.

CHELSEA BROWN WATCHED as Walton pulled out of the parking lot and drove away. He was sore; she could tell from his stride, but the set to his shoulders was also indicative of something else. She walked into the bar moments later, here to pick up her brother, but she stopped in the corner for a moment and stared at the group. She was a bit hidden, out of their line of sight, seeing the same men she'd watched playing earlier today, and heard part of their conversation. Apparently Walton was the center of attention.

"You know we can't keep babying him," Brian said in disgust.

Johnny frowned. "It's not as if we're babying him, for crying out loud. We're just playing a game."

"You think so? What are you, blind? It's not as much a game as a pity party."

Chelsea winced at that. Who with any pride would take that comment in good stead? This was Walton they were talking about, and he was stubborn, more so than a lot of men she knew. It went along with being military as well as dealing with his injuries, she assumed. Yet Walton was determined to work damn hard on his mobility. It would be a shame if these guys' attitudes set him back.

As she walked toward her brother, Stan looked up and smiled, standing now. "Here's my chauffeur. I'll talk to you guys later."

Stan eyed her as they walked out. "What was that look on your face for?" he asked curiously.

"Were you guys talking about Walton?"

He winced. "Right. He was one of your patients, wasn't he?"

"I saw him outside, and he looked pretty ragged."

"It was a pretty rough soccer game today," he pointed out.

"Yeah, and that was definitely part of the physical effects I could see with Walton, but that stiffness to his neck and shoulders just means he was holding back something pretty emotional."

Stan groaned. "That's the problem with living in a small town. You get to know *everything* about *everybody*."

"Yeah, I also know what he's been going through."

"Which is why we play with him."

"But what you're saying is you're only playing with him because of pity, … not because he's any good."

"He was good," Stan pointed out. "He was incredible, and everybody wants nothing more than for him to be good again."

"Point noted. Yet he's not good anymore. Is that what you're saying?"

"I'm not saying that he can't be good. I don't know that. However, I'm not sure that he can improve because of the missing leg," he muttered, fumbling over his words. "I don't know what the deal is. You would have a better understanding than me, but the guys want to get into a league. We have to set up a team roster to play. If we ever get there, we need to be more competitive. If that happens, Walton will really struggle."

"You mean, *you guys* will struggle," she stated, calling a spade a spade. She'd never been one to pussyfoot around when it came to the truth.

"Maybe," Stan conceded, with a shrug. "I don't care because I play for fun, but some of the guys are a little more serious when it comes to that level of play."

She nodded. "You're talking about Brian, I presume?"

He glanced at her and agreed. "Yeah, Brian's always been very competitive."

"And he always wants to win, no matter the cost," she added. "I remember that very well."

Stan laughed. "Of course you do. You were fighting with him all through high school and college."

"No, I left for college," she clarified, raising her hand, "and he was one of the reasons."

"It doesn't matter what the reason was. The thing is, Brian remains very competitive."

She nodded and dropped it.

"Do you know anything about War Dogs?" Stan asked suddenly.

She frowned at him. "No. What are you talking about? As in the military ones that go to war?"

"Yeah, apparently the US has a large Department of War Dogs, and the ones that retire get adopted out," he explained. "I didn't even know anything about it, not until Walton mentioned it."

"I wonder why he brought that up?" she muttered.

"I think he's been asked to look into one that's gone missing locally."

She shook her head. "He sure as hell isn't ready to go back to work."

"I don't think it's paid work. It's a temporary gig. I think it's more of a friends-and-favor thing."

"Ah." Chelsea nodded. "Maybe that'll give him something to think about other than you guys." She winced at her own waspish tone because she knew not to handle this in that way. Yet she hated to see anybody hurt, and she knew that some damage had already been done.

Whether it was just to Walton's pride or not, she didn't know. If it was, that was a good thing because some wounds would heal. However, if it went deeper to a self-esteem issue of not being good enough, then it would be a whole different story. "Those hurtful comments could really set back

Walton's progress," she muttered, "especially if he believes you guys."

"What's to believe, Chelsea? If he can't play soccer, he can't play soccer," Stan declared. "We can't make that happen for him."

"No, but that doesn't mean that other people can't make it happen for him," she pointed out, "and he's working so hard, and you guys giving him a chance would make a huge difference."

"We did, and this wasn't the first time we've played with him either," Stan added. "We've played with him every Sunday."

"Is he getting any better?"

He hesitated, then shrugged. "I'm not sure."

"And that would mean *no*." Her shoulders sagged, as she recognized the looming reality of Walton's losing one of the sports that he'd always loved.

"He can still play at practice," Stan suggested.

"Not likely," she pointed out. "He'll just feel as if he doesn't belong."

"We can't make everybody's life happen," Stan muttered. "I know you want to take on the world and to save everybody, but sometimes that just doesn't work."

Those were definitely words of truth, which she had to accept as she dropped off Stan at his place and headed home. It was a truth that she didn't always want to see, but she was forced to deal with reality, given her line of work. With patients recovering from some of the most incredible injuries, as long as they continued to improve, then she was happy. But it didn't take much to set back their progress, and people being less than kind with their words or actions was a sure way to do that. Walton's case was a different one.

This group of guys had been playing together for a long time. Walton was part of the group, but that was before he had gone away to serve in the military.

As a matter of fact, he had been gone for quite a few years. They couldn't expect him to be the same after these injuries, and he couldn't expect to be at his full potential after suffering the loss of a leg and two fingers. She headed to the grocery store to grab a few things and saw him again.

He stood in front of the meat department, staring at the shelf but obviously not seeing it.

She walked up and nudged him. "Earth to Walton. Earth to Walton."

Startled, he turned to her and shrugged. "Not sure Earth is a place I want to be just now."

She schooled her expression because she understood exactly what he meant. "Tough day on the soccer field, *huh?*"

"Yeah, for sure," he admitted, regaining his usual smile.

"I picked up Stan and took him home. He mentioned something about a War Dog."

He eyed her with interest. "Do you know anything about them?"

"Nope, I sure don't."

"Have you heard of anybody here having one?"

"No, nothing," she replied.

He raised both hands in frustration. "That's not helpful."

She laughed. "You could always check with the local veterinarians though."

"One of the guys suggested that," he noted. "I thought I would go home and make some phone calls."

She nodded. "You're not trying to go back to work or anything yet, are you?"

"It's not that I'm *trying* to go back to work, but the woman who looks after my prosthetic asked me if I was up to looking into the lost dog."

Chelsea nodded, feeling relief inside her. "Good. I'm sure that will keep you interested in life."

"Do I look as if I'm not interested in life?"

She smiled up at him. "There are a lot of ways to be interested and a lot of ways to *not* be."

"Oh boy, here we go again with the psychobabble."

"Hardly psychobabble," she protested.

"Sometimes I think you should have gotten your psych degree," he teased.

"Sometimes I think about that too, and other times I think about leaving here and never coming back," she admitted, with a laugh.

"You've been threatening to do that since you were in high school. And you did go away to college. Yet here you are back again." He motioned at the steaks in front of him. "I don't know where I'll be traveling to as I look for the dog, or if any travel will be involved. Presumably I'll have to ensure it's the right dog at some point."

"You've got to find it first," she noted, then pointed to the meat case. "Heavy protein is good for you when you're rebuilding, and you put out quite a bit of energy on the field today."

He nodded agreeably and seemed to be happy to let that topic slide.

They went their separate ways in the store, and she picked up the rest of her groceries, then found herself going through the checkout lines with him at the same time.

He raised his eyebrows. "You got that done pretty fast."

"Yeah, I didn't need much. I'm not doing a whole lot of

cooking these days."

He smirked. "Don't forget that protein is important."

She snorted. "Right, as if I'll take advice from you." Still grinning, she headed out to her car. As she stowed away her groceries, she noted that he was parked only a few vehicles away.

Just then his phone rang, and he put it on Speakerphone, unloading his purchases as he spoke.

Chelsea couldn't help but hear somebody on the other end, somebody named Kat.

His tone warmed considerably as he talked to her.

Chelsea frowned at that, not sure why it would upset her, beyond the fact that she'd always liked Walton and had wondered multiple times about inviting him out for coffee or something. However, she had been waiting until they were no longer patient and therapist. Still, that time had come and gone.

He only came in for occasional checkups nowadays, instead of regular treatments. She wasn't aware he had somebody of interest already, until the topic of the War Dog came up, and she figured that Kat was his prosthetic lady. As Chelsea recalled, the woman lived somewhere in New Mexico.

Chelsea didn't want to listen in, yet it was hard not to. She walked a little bit closer and waited until he got off. When he looked at her, one eyebrow raised, she asked, "Good news?"

He shrugged. "Probably not. I needed details on the dog, and she was giving me the rundown. I don't want to slog my way through everything, and she was hoping I'd gotten somewhere already."

"But you haven't had a chance to even ask anybody yet,

except for me and the guys."

"Right, but Kat's definitely an eyes-on-the-ball kind of person," he shared, with a big smile.

"Sounds as if you really like her."

"She's pretty amazing," he replied, his tone warming up again.

"Is she married?" Chelsea asked in a teasing tone.

"Married? More like happily married," he replied, laughing. "Badger's also in the same boat."

"What do you mean by *the same boat*?" she asked, curious now.

"Kat's missing a leg, and so is Badger." When she stared at him in surprise, he nodded. "It goes along with our world, though at the moment it still seems as if my world has completely shifted," he shared, as he glanced back at the grocery store. Yet she got the feeling he was thinking back to the post-game scenario at the bar.

"I'm not sure a shift is necessarily a bad thing," she noted briskly, as she turned and headed back to her car. "Let me know if you get anywhere on that War Dog thing."

"Why?" he asked curiously. "Last I heard you weren't particularly fond of dogs."

She pivoted, frowning at him. "Oh no, I've always loved animals. It was my mother who couldn't stand being around them."

"I'm afraid that the War Dog might be at one of the hunting lodges. And, being a War Dog, plus retired at that, he's most likely injured. I sure don't want him in any situations where he would be outmatched."

"Don't forget. If you need any help with hunting lodges or have questions, … there's always Rick."

"Rick?"

"My older brother, remember?"

He studied her and then nodded. "That could be pretty helpful."

"I can give him a shout, if you want." She pulled out her phone and waved it in front of him.

He nodded. "If you wouldn't mind, that would be great."

She quickly placed a call, hoping that maybe there would be some cell access. Her brother often couldn't be reached, depending on the weather and the satellite and how frozen the sole cell tower was, but this time she got lucky. "Hey, bro," she greeted him in a playful tone.

"Look at that. My little sis is calling. What's up?" he asked.

"You remember Walton?"

"Of course I remember Walton."

"He's here with me right now."

"Oh, now that's an interesting twist." His tone turned teasing.

She rolled her eyes. "He's been asked to look into a retired War Dog that's supposed to be here somewhere, maybe in your neck of the woods. Apparently the government does welfare checks on the dogs periodically, and Walton's been asked to help, but they don't have a good handle on where this one is."

"A War Dog, *huh*?" Rick asked. "That's interesting."

"Why? What's interesting?"

"Because I just heard one of the four guests I have up here talking about a War Dog."

"What did they say?" Walton leaned forward, so his voice could be heard on the phone.

"Hey, Walton. Nice to hear from you. I haven't seen you

in forever. I hear you came back minus a body part."

"Minus a few of them," he replied a bit stiffly, "but that's old news. Tell me about this War Dog."

"They mentioned something about training or taking a War Dog out hunting. One of the guys figured it might be a good match between grizzlies and the dog."

"What the hell?" Walton asked briskly, as he stared down at the phone. "He wasn't serious about using the dog to flush out grizzlies, was he?"

"Honestly, the way he was talking, it sounded a whole lot worse than that. When I went to question them, they all just told me that he was joking."

"Interesting."

"If you don't want him here flushing out grizzlies, quite possibly testing the dog, you might want to get your ass up here and look at him."

"You've got the dog there?"

"Definitely one is here," Rick confirmed. "Can't swear it's the one you're after, but it seems more likely than not."

"Any chance you could shoot me a photo of it?"

"I can do that. May take me a bit though, given our situation with the cell tower and satellite and whatnot. I don't know how long it'll take."

"I would appreciate it if you could. I would hate to make the trip if it's not the dog I'm looking for."

"I highly doubt that more than one War Dog is up here, but who knows," Rick replied. "Give me a little bit, and I'll send it to my sister." And, with that, he ended the call.

Chelsea looked over at him. "As soon as I get the photo, I'll forward it to you."

"Good enough, thanks." Walton smiled and nodded. "That was a good idea. I'll still need his phone number because I want a little more information on the men up there."

She gave it to him, quickly sending it in a text, then looked at him. "They really wouldn't do something like that with the dog, would they?"

"I would hope not," Walton muttered, "but people act differently when they find out it's a War Dog."

"*Right.*" She visibly shuddered. "I hope these guys aren't of that same ilk."

"Who knows," Walton replied, with a shrug. "Yet, if they are, you can bet that isn't what the War Department had planned for the dog's retirement."

"And yet how much control do they have?" she asked. "I mean, once they hand over the dog, and it's been adopted, how much control of what happens to a War Dog do they really have?"

"I don't know," Walton admitted, "but you can be sure that I'll have something to say about it."

She winced. "You won't go up there, will you?"

"I will if I need to," he stated, with conviction. "Besides, your brother said that they were up there now, right?"

"He offered to take a picture of him, so I would presume so." She quickly sent her brother a text to confirm that but got no response. "He probably has no service right now," she said, with a shrug.

"Of course not. That would make things way too easy," Walton muttered, as he stared down at their phones. "I guess I'll contact Kat again and see what she has to say about it."

"I would prefer you didn't go up there and put that added stress on your leg. However, if you need to go, I've got a few days off coming up, so I could go with you," she offered impulsively. When he turned and frowned at her, she shrugged. "I've been up to my brother's lodge, but that was years ago, before Dad got so sick. I wouldn't want to go alone, and my schedule has never worked out with anyone else's. But, if you're heading up there to check out the dog, I would be happy to go along."

"How long of a drive is it?" he asked.

"About six hours."

He thought about it and nodded. "It would be easier with two of us. I haven't driven that far lately."

"Meaning, your leg won't handle it?"

"I don't know everything about what my leg can handle," he stated bluntly, "but, if you're up for the trip and want a few days away and a chance to see your brother, it works for me."

CHAPTER 2

LATER ON THAT evening, now at home, Chelsea wondered at her offer out of the blue. She meant it, and she had intended to get back to her brother's lodge at some point but definitely didn't want to go alone. It wasn't exactly the place for her, though she knew that she was safe from any unwanted male attention just because it was her brother's place. Yet a hunting lodge and armed men killing animals wasn't a place she expected to feel all that comfortable. Rick had been bugging her to visit for a long time, so this would be a perfect excuse. Yet Walton still had to know if it was the right animal. And, even if it was the right dog, what would they do about it?

She sighed as she headed up for a shower, contemplating this situation, which was definitely on the strange side. But she did have several days off coming up, which she took on an annual basis, and she hadn't made any plans yet. In fact, she hadn't even had a clue what she wanted to do with her time off. Holidays were one of those things that she tended to spend at home doing nothing, which was even more depressing. She could make a trip down south to visit some old friends, but her not making plans was almost like she'd known something else would come up because she had deliberately left her calendar free.

When Walton called her about 11:00 p.m., he greeted

her, saying, "Sorry for the late call."

"It's okay. I'm just getting ready for bed."

"I was afraid you might be asleep already."

"No, not yet," she murmured. "What's up?"

"I ended up texting your brother, asking for a bit more information on the guy and whatnot, so he sent the dog's photo directly to me. I've confirmed with Kat and Badger that it does appear to be the War Dog that I'm looking for."

"Oh, so does that mean you need to go, or you don't know yet?"

"I explained the little bit that your brother had shared, and Kat's not too impressed with the War Dog's current situation. The dog was supposed to be with a retired veteran, as a companion dog."

"Ah, I wonder if maybe the original adopter died or something, and the dog was handed off."

"That's possible, but it also means that this particular War Dog wasn't necessarily vetted for this adoption. Kat and Badger are also worried that something murky was in the original application process to begin with."

"Meaning, the guy might have lied?"

Such a note of disgust filled her tone that both her and Walton laughed. "Yeah, and, as we know, people do lie all the time."

"You're not kidding," she grumbled. "So what's the answer?"

"I'll go take a look to ensure the dog's okay."

"Yet you know that, if this guy does have the dog, and the situation isn't okay, you'll have a hell of a fight taking it away from him. These hunters are heavily armed."

Walton sighed. "I also got the names of your brother's guests," he added, "and that raised some alarms as well."

"Why?"

"Because … Kat ran a quick background check on all of them, and this one guy from Mississippi raises red flags."

Chelsea had to wonder how they could run a quick check on somebody that fast.

"The guy's a sleazeball, and he's been questioned for a shooting back there."

"A shooting, of a human?" Her heart sank as she thought about it. "That means, … no, I don't even know what that means."

"Neither do I, but believe me. It makes my hair stand on end."

"Sure, but that's got nothing to do with the War Dog, right? It's not as if he used the dog to kill somebody, right?"

"True. This guy died by gunshot. However, if this Chad guy is already in a police database, he could be a repeat offender."

"If so, can he even legally have a gun? What about any consequences of violating his bail or probation or whatever? What hits me the most is, if he's a current suspect, why would the cops allow him to just up and leave Mississippi and come all the way out here to Alaska?"

"He had friends here and wanted to get out of town, presumably how he came in contact with the War Dog. Apparently the hunting trip holiday had been planned for a while, and the authorities knew where he would be so without any reason to charge him, had nothing against his leaving."

"Interesting," she murmured. "I guess, just because he's being questioned, it doesn't mean the cops can prove he did it. He's just an active suspect."

"Still, makes him a viable candidate. Kat phoned the

department and explained what the issue was. They said that Chad's got a penchant for violence, so they're keeping an eye on him. In the meantime, they don't have any other evidence, so they're more or less just biding their time."

"That sucks," she said. "Did they say who died?"

"Yeah, someone from their group of friends."

"Friends up there hunting with Chad now?"

"More of the same group, only they all stayed there while this guy 'moved' up here for a few months knowing the hunting trip was still going ahead and wanting to get away for a bit," Walton confirmed. "It seems they all were in the same group and are also under suspicion."

"I don't know what you make of it, but that sounds dodgy as hell," she muttered.

"So, I am going up to your brother's place, but I don't think you should come with me."

She stiffened and glared at the phone. "Now hang on a minute."

"Did you hear what I just said about their tendency for violence?"

"Yeah, I heard you, but I also heard you say that they were under suspicion. ... That's not the same thing as being guilty."

"True, but I don't want to knowingly bring you into a scenario that potentially could get ugly."

"And yet it's my brother's place. So, if it'll get ugly, he'll be right there in the middle of it."

"Yes, that's true, but I don't know what else might happen. ... Still, I can't stop you from going."

"No, you can't," she snapped, cutting him off. "And remember that, because of me, you are even looking to go in the first place."

"Yes, but I don't want you to feel as if you have to go now, just because you made the offer earlier. You didn't have all the facts beforehand."

"Let's get something clear," she explained. "I have five days off work, and I have to take them soon. I've wanted to go to my brother's for a while now, but I didn't really want to go alone. This seems to be the perfect opportunity."

"It also could turn into a *perfect* mess," Walton pointed out. "And I might have to leave soon after finding the dog."

"We'll deal with that later. Look. I'll tell my brother that I'm coming with you and that we're leaving tomorrow morning."

"Really?" he asked, with a note of amusement. "Are you always this *take-chargey?*"

"You should know that already," she replied, "since I've been dealing with you constantly."

"You have, but not in the last six or eight weeks."

"Maybe not," she conceded, "but that's because you're at the point where you don't need me to *babysit* you."

"No, I certainly don't need babysitting," he snapped.

She laughed. "Oh, this will be a great trip. You can pick me up at seven."

"Make it six," he replied, ending the call.

And, with that, she glared at the phone. Yet she was oddly excited. Not about meeting a group of armed men under suspicion for murder, but about going on a road trip with Walton. She felt great.

She'd considered the idea of contacting him so many times, yet it never really seemed appropriate. She also wanted to ensure that he was feeling better and getting over his injuries before she reached out in a more personal way. Yet she was waiting for him to check in with her, which made no sense because she generally wasn't somebody who would wait.

Shrugging, she sent her brother a quick text, asking if there was room for two more. He called her. "Are you coming with Walton?"

"Ah, you already know he's coming?"

"Yep, I sure do," Rick replied. "It's kind of a weird thing."

"I know, but his going to visit you is one of the reasons I wanted to come," she explained.

"He did tell me that these guys are under suspicion, but they weren't charged, at least not right now," he pointed out.

"To be honest, all kinds of things could have happened, and those guys may not have any idea what was going on. They might be completely innocent."

"Maybe," Rick conceded, "but it's rough up here already, as you well know."

"Of course it is. I'm not looking to be babysat," she muttered into the phone. "You've been hassling me to come up for a long time, and now here I'm coming, and all you're doing is trying to chase me away."

He laughed. "Sis, I'll never chase you away. If you do come, I want you to be safe."

"Now you sound like Walton. He's trying to talk me out of it too, but how unsafe can it be?" she retorted. "I mean, I've got you looking after me. Plus, Walton will be there every step of the way too."

And, with that, she quickly ended the call, packed, and, in almost no time, had her bag at the front door. She was hoping Walton wouldn't pull one over on her and leave her behind. She would have something to say about that and would contact her brother. Yet she also knew that she could do little to stop Walton from leaving her here.

Early that next morning, with everything checked out again before she was good to go, she stepped out onto the front step, just to see Walton pulling up. She waved at him as she carried her bag down. "Good timing," she greeted him cheerfully. He nodded, got out, and helped her with her bag. "I forgot you had this big truck. This will be perfect for going up there."

"Same truck I've always had," he said, with a note of humor. "Got it when I was in high school. I keep it in the garage most of the time and just bring it out when it's the right tool for the job. I've always kept my vehicles in the best condition I can."

"Unlike a lot of guys," she noted, with an eye roll, "who treat their trucks like crap."

"Hey, I understand what a blessing a well-oiled machine is," he shared, "and I fight the lack of it every day."

Realizing what he meant on a personal level, she nodded. "The good news is that you're still fighting, and the human body is pretty miraculous, and that's all good."

"Is it?" he asked, with a note of humor. "Sometimes it feels as if I might still be fighting, but I already lost the war."

"Maybe, and maybe the war was something you needed to lose," she replied, knowing that he probably wouldn't understand—or wouldn't *want* to understand. Still, she was unable to help herself from poking and prodding a little bit more. When he looked over at her, she shrugged. "Sometimes people fight to the extent that they're just blinded to what the reality is."

"And yet, if you give in to the reality," he pointed out, "you'll never change it."

She smiled. "I think it's a compromise between the two

that needs to happen," she murmured. "I've seen too many guys completely deny where they are at, and then they go out and do way too much, sometimes making things way worse."

"Of course," he admitted. "That's human nature."

"Is it?" she muttered. "And here I thought it was just … *men*'s nature." He burst out laughing at that, and she grinned broadly. "I do like the sound of your laughter," she said impulsively. When he stared at her, she shrugged, then climbed into the passenger seat. "Sorry, apparently that was the wrong thing to say."

Walton shook his head. "No, it wasn't wrong at all. I haven't heard the sound of my own laughter a whole lot recently either," he murmured, his voice deep.

"And yet you've been getting so much better."

"I have," he agreed, with a smile, as he settled in the driver's seat.

So much better that he was obviously considering his work options coming up. She knew about his ambitions. "How's the wood carving going for you?"

"It's starting to make a little bit of money," he shared, with a wry look in her direction, "but it could be a little tough to make a living off of."

"I'm not so sure about that," she noted. "Maybe you just need some publicity, some marketing, and that might be something I could help you with." When he frowned at her, she shrugged. "I always find myself getting bored."

"*Bored*," he repeated. "You already work full-time."

"I know, but I used to work full-time as well as take care of my sick father, and now he's gone." Her voice caught in the back of her throat.

"Right. Now that he's gone, it's hard to fill that hole in your time, isn't it?"

"It's brutal," she agreed. "Obviously a little publicity work wouldn't be a permanent thing. It just might be a bit of a challenge to see if I can make something happen for you."

"You're welcome to try," Walton replied, with a shrug. "It's not as if anybody knows who or what I am and what I do."

"They just need to see your carvings. Your stuff is fantastic," she said, while frowning at him.

"Even so, it's still hard to do any mass production with hand carvings by a sole artist."

"Which is why you don't want anything that requires that level of production," she scolded. "Your stuff is one of a kind, and plenty of people out there would be willing to pay for it and would appreciate the time involved in creating such a piece. We just need to find them."

He smiled. "Hey, look, if you can find people willing to pay for my pieces, it will make me a very happy man. It's just that simple."

She laughed. "Maybe while we're driving, we could discuss a marketing plan then. How many pieces do you have done?"

He shrugged. "I'm not sure. I don't know how many of them are sellable."

"They're *all* sellable," she declared.

He rolled his eyes. "I am getting better as I go along."

"We all do," she stated, grinning at him. "This trip will be fun."

"Says you," he muttered. "I'm not at all sure I'm fully prepared for it."

"No, maybe not," she said, "but that's okay."

"How come you're not helping your brother with his

marketing stuff?"

"I was, but then he got married, and Julie took it over."

"Ah, was that an issue between you two?"

"No, not at all. Back then our father was pretty ill, and I didn't have time for marketing for Rick anyway."

"That makes sense. Does he come back home for the winter?"

"Yeah, but then, as he gets bookings, he has to go back out again. Rick's always back and forth. Plus, he's also on call a lot. As you may know, he's got the volunteer fire department gig too here at home," she pointed out, rolling her eyes. "We keep pretty busy."

"Yet here you are, still looking to get busier."

She thought about it for a long moment, then nodded. "Yeah, but I can stand to be a little bit busier."

"As long as it's just a little bit because I can't pay you," he warned.

"I didn't ask for payment," she declared, staring at him.

"I know, but most people prefer to get paid for their time. It's a thing."

"Yeah, I get it, but, on this deal, I don't even know if I can make anything happen."

"But didn't you help your brother get out the message on his hunting lodge?"

"Yep, I sure did, and then I taught his wife, Julie, what to do to carry it on."

"Good, so maybe you do know something about it."

Recognizing that he was teasing, Chelsea laughed. "More than I used to anyway. I cut my teeth on my brother's business, and I really had no clue what I was doing, but I learned fast because he needed customers. It's hard to maintain a business up here in the wilds if you don't have a steady clientele."

"Everybody needs regulars," Walton agreed, "but, along with the regulars, you also need paying customers."

"That was half the problem, as Rick was dropping the prices to entice people in. Then, when they would come, he was putting on quite the spread, trying to keep them, which cost him quite a bit. Meanwhile, he was barely putting food on his own table. It's been hard to find a balance."

"Yeah, finding the balance is the key to most things, I would think."

"It is," she agreed, "so we can work on some of that with you too."

"If you want to, sure. I won't say no to the help."

"Good, because I wouldn't let you stop me." Again he burst out laughing, and she grinned. "I think that'll be my job these next few days. Making you laugh as much as possible."

"Good Lord," he muttered, as he stared at her. "It's nice to know that some laughter is in my world again, but I was getting there just fine."

"You were," she agreed, with a shrug, "but sometimes you just need a little bit of encouragement."

"A little bit, but if you're planning on making me laugh all weekend, I won't get any work done."

She asked him, "What work do you think you'll do up there?"

"Why don't you tell me," he said, "and we'll see if we're on the same page."

"You'll check out if the dog is really the right War Dog. Then presumably, knowing you, you'll confirm that the dog is in good shape," she stated.

"Good shape and living a good life," he added, with a

nod.

"Do you really think that is part of the parameters that Kat is asking of you?"

"Too damn bad if it's not," he stated, "because I could no more leave an animal to be abused than I could a person. It's just not in me. And, by the way, it's not in Kat either, and Badger even more so."

"Ah, got it. But if it's this guy's animal …"

"Then he should have proof that it's his animal, shouldn't he?"

"*Hmm*, I guess the government has quite a selection process for these adoptions, don't they?"

"They sure do," he noted, with a smile. "So the sooner we get there and see who these guys are, the better."

"But …"

"But what?"

"I just don't want to cause my brother any hardship. Rick has had his fair share of problems, and I don't want to dump any others on him."

"Of course not," Walton agreed. "He shouldn't suffer any hardship. These guys on the cops' radar? … Remember that they haven't been charged. They were just questioned in regard to a murder."

"Of one of their own friends," she pointed out.

"Yep, I got more details sent my way this morning and looked it over when I got up."

"Interesting," she noted, "so the cops are looking at the entire group?"

"They were all together at the time, and a fight broke out between them. The fight was broken up, then everybody headed home. This Rudy guy was found on the wayside, outside of his vehicle. He'd been shot."

"Oh, ouch, that fight scene right beforehand makes it that much more difficult for these guys."

"Makes it much more of a challenge to walk away from them as suspects," he added.

"And the thing is," Chelsea added, "with everybody up at Rick's retreat, for all you know, they were all in on Rudy's death."

He stared at her, then shook his head. "Not likely. If too many people know, too many can rat out the others."

"Okay, so maybe not likely," she conceded, as she thought about it. "Yet, if they all know each other and have been friends for a long time, you can bet they have a pretty good idea what happened."

"I would think the police have that in mind too," he pointed out.

"Sure, but that doesn't mean the local authorities in Alaska or in Mississippi have the manpower or the capacity to follow these guys all the time."

"I don't imagine they do," Walton agreed, with a nod.

Chelsea sighed. "On the other hand, the Mississippi cops didn't stop this group from going on a hunting trip in Alaska? Weren't they told to stay in touch? So, when the guys told the cops about the hunting trip, the cops were fine with it?"

"Supposedly," Walton replied.

"Yeah, they're fine with it, until somebody else turns up dead," she muttered.

He took his gaze off the road to glance at her. "Why would you say that?" he asked, studying her intently.

She shook her head. "If somebody does know what happened with Rudy, and a falling out among thieves happened once, there could easily be a second falling out. I just hope no one else turns up dead."

WALTON FROWNED. CHELSEA had brought up an interesting point. "It sounds as if you've made a study of crime somewhere along the line."

She shrugged. "I guess I'm kind of a crime buff," she confessed, "but that doesn't make me too weird, does it?"

"No, I find it interesting, given your profession."

"I think that's what sent me searching for answers. I see so many people after accidents, but sometimes they're not accidents, but intentional injuries. It makes me wonder what goes on with humanity that they would do such things to each other."

"Ah, that makes sense in a way too."

She shrugged. "We don't always know how to respond to a lot of things in life, and certainly an awful lot happens that doesn't make any sense," she acknowledged, with a wry smile. "This is definitely the kind of thing that never makes any sense. At least not to me."

"Of course not," he murmured. "When you think about it, so much about human nature leaves us guessing. Consider all the mass shootings, family annihilators, greed killings, serial killers, human trafficking, and all the rest. People do so many unthinkable things to each other that you wonder what they were thinking."

"Not only what were they thinking, but some of the injuries that they leave on their victims who survive are just awful," she noted. "I'm working with several patients, and what they've gone through is just … brutal."

He glanced at her again from the driver's seat and nodded. "I can't imagine thinking like a murderer or an abuser."

"Right." Chelsea shook her head. "Nobody ever does, unless they're involved somehow. For me, as a physiotherapist, I'm obviously dealing with the after-effects. We've got one guy we're treating now, and his brother killed everybody in the family. When it came around to my patient, his brother just shot him up. He didn't kill him, so he's dealing with part of his face now missing. Plus, his shoulder muscles were just chopped to ribbons. It all seemed to be without any rhyme or reason."

"So, this was somebody who really angered him?"

"I guess. It's one of the cases that sent me trying to understand basic human behavior. Obviously we take some psychology courses in my line of work, but, even with a good education, you don't really understand until you are faced with some of these atrocities. All too frequently, we never reach an understanding of that kind of evil."

"That's true." And they launched into a much deeper discussion. Thankfully that conversation morphed back into marketing his carvings, which was a relief. Before he realized it, they were taking the turnoff to the lodge.

Following the deep, dark roads into the forest, he smiled. "It's been a really long time since I've been up here."

"Have you ever been here before, to Rick's lodge?"

"No, nothing in this particular area, but I have been in lots of similar places nearby," he replied, with a smile. "Something is very freeing about it."

"I always found it kind of … I guess I'll have to find the right word. For some it's *freeing*, but, for me? Being out in the wild with no civilization around, it's … *claustrophobic*." When he stared at her, she shrugged. It made no sense to others, but, for her, it was clear. She was pretty sure it was all connected to the fact that she had no cell phone service or any reliable mode of communication in the area. She would be totally cut off here.

"I was pretty young the last time I was at the lodge, which is another reason my brother has been trying hard to get me to come back," she explained, all with a smile. "I found myself troubled by the fact that I couldn't contact anybody, couldn't reach out, and, instead of it being freeing, it was limiting and honestly frightening."

"Which explains the claustrophobia," Walton noted, with a shrug. "Interesting how we're all so different." It took another good twenty minutes of backroad driving before they finally pulled up to the lodge. He looked at it and nodded. "Wow, it seems Rick has done pretty well for himself."

She smiled. "I did say I was doing the marketing."

He burst out laughing. "If this is part of your portfolio that you wanted to show me, then you're more than welcome to do what you can for my humble little carving operation."

She grinned. "Thank you, and I'll be happy to. It will be a new challenge, and I could do well with a challenge." She hopped out of the truck, then walked around to the back and pulled out their bags. She put them down as the double front doors opened, and two dogs bounded out, barking like crazy until they saw her, and then they were all over her, looking for loving cuddles. "Look at this," she muttered, chuckling, "if it isn't Tweedledum and Tweedledee."

"How do you tell them apart?" Walton asked, eyeing the two large red Irish setters.

"I can't," she replied. "That's why I call them that."

"You mean, that's not their names?"

"No, that's not their names," snapped a woman with an exasperated tone standing in the doorway. "They have perfectly good names that Chelsea continually refuses to use." She then burst out laughing.

Chelsea pointed out, "Then they should be easy to tell apart, which they aren't, assuming they even know their names, which they don't."

"Thank you. That is true, but Chelsea's never managed to tell them apart since they were little." The woman came down the steps and held out her hand. "Hi, I'm Julie, Rick's wife."

He shook her hand and smiled at her. "I feel as if I know you from high school."

She groaned. "That's the problem with being a local," she stated. "Everybody knows you from a long time ago, even if it's things you would just as soon they don't remember."

He noted, "I have only the gentlest of memories."

She burst out laughing. "Thank you for that much," she murmured. She grinned at Chelsea. "Look what it finally took to get you back here."

"But, hey, I'm here." Chelsea sighed. "Though there are no guarantees I'm staying, mind you. How are the bugs?" she asked Julie, with a wince.

"Heavy. They always are. Especially in the evenings when outside, but they're not that bad once you're inside."

"Right, I'm pretty sure my brother lied to me about that last time too."

Julie laughed. "Come on in."

As they walked up the front steps, the two dogs followed happily. Walton smiled at them. "Social dogs."

"You need that kind here," Julie explained. "You also

need dogs capable of handling themselves because we do get the wildlife here too."

"Sure, but nothing can handle all the wildlife," he stated, looking at her.

"True, and that's what I meant about the dogs handling themselves. They need to know when it's time to run and to not pick a fight they don't need to be picking. Plus, they stick together. These two do love to be outside, so they only come home to eat and sleep. You should be impressed that they were here to meet you," Julie said. "Let me show you to your rooms, and then you can come on down for coffee. Rick should be in shortly. He took the hunting group to scout some areas that might be good for them."

Walton nodded. "Good enough." As they walked upstairs to the rooms, he was surprised and yet somehow not surprised that their rooms were connecting. As Julie left them to their own devices, Walton looked over at Chelsea, with an eyebrow raised.

She shrugged. "Sorry. I told them that I was coming up with you. It just didn't occur to me—"

"You *did* come up with me. I wasn't expecting this type of *personal* service, however."

She snorted. "No, and don't count on getting it again either," she muttered, "because, when it comes to me, it's hit and miss with them."

"But I don't want Rick to get the impression that we're together."

"Hence, the door between us, I think."

"Good," he replied, with a smirk. "The last thing I want is your brother all over me about *my intentions.*"

She burst out laughing. "If he does go down that pathway, you send him to me. We had quite the argument when he married Julie because I dared to ask questions, which he didn't appreciate."

"Of course not," he said, "you were the little sister."

"Yeah, but I was asking because of our father," she explained, with a wry smile. "Believe me that the translation from Papa to younger sister didn't go well."

Walton was still grinning when he entered the huge dining room area, where off to the side was the coffeepot. "As long as I get free coffee, I'm good," he muttered. Then he hesitated and asked Chelsea, "Did you have a special pricing deal with your brother?"

"I don't have to pay," she shared. "I'll talk to him about yours."

"It's fine," Walton said, with a wave of his hand. "I can pay."

"Is this paid for by your people or the government?"

He frowned at that and shrugged. "I'm not sure it is. This is a volunteer gig, and I think my expenses are paid, to a limit. Kat asked me for a favor, and I just agreed and didn't ask any further questions, so I have no idea."

"Of course you would do a volunteer thing," she replied, staring at him.

"Anyway, that arrangement is for me to deal with," he declared, with a bright smile, "and don't you worry. I've got money."

"I know, but this stuff is expensive."

He shrugged. "I'm certainly not asking your brother for charity."

"No, of course you aren't." She glared at him. "You wouldn't."

"No, I wouldn't," he confirmed, returning the glare.

"Come on, you two. Now I know you're together," Julie

interceded, with a smile. "Nothing quite gets our goat than the significant other person in our world."

"Yeah, let's put that to rest once and for all. We're not *together*-together," Chelsea pointed out.

Julie nodded. "I can see that. You haven't quite gotten that far yet, but there's still hope." She looked at Walton sideways. "Chelsea has told us a fair bit about you."

"Oh, *great*, thanks." Chelsea raised both hands in frustration. "As if I really wanted him to know that."

Julie burst out laughing. "Oh, this will be fun, and your brother will rag on you nonstop. You had to be expecting that."

"He can just knock it off before he starts," Chelsea stated. "He runs me way too ragged as it is."

"Ha," Rick greeted them, as he walked into the room, his arms opened wide, giving his baby sister a big hug. "I don't run you ragged at all. By rights, I should be giving you shit and raking this guy over the coals already." He walked over and shook Walton's hand. "Nice to see you."

He nodded. "Likewise."

They studied each other, and Rick nodded. "You were a couple years behind me in school, as I recall."

"Probably," he agreed easily. "I was a year ahead of Chelsea."

"Ah." Rick gave a knowing nod in her direction.

She glared at him. "What the hell does that mean?"

"Nothing," he said, with an innocent smile.

She groaned and added, "Okay, you guys need to knock it off. You are making me uncomfortable. We're not *together*-together."

"Right. I heard that," Rick noted, "but, from the sounds of it, you're well on the way." Rick gave her another big hug and then nudged her a little closer to Walton. "I would prefer that you not bring up anything about the court case," he told them. "I understand these men are here to have a bonding experience after the death of their friend, especially now that an investigation and a legal matter have put a lot of pressure on their relationship."

"Something like losing one of their group would do that," Chelsea stated.

"Exactly, so they're here for fun and games, not necessarily any stressful things, so I don't really want you messing it up." He glanced back at Walton. "What are you supposed to do if the dog isn't his?"

"One thing's for certain. The dog *isn't* his, and I can tell you that right now. The War Dog had been cleared and adopted by an older retired veteran the government is trying to get a hold of right now. They are already working on trying to confirm who picked up the War Dog from his legal owner."

"What if the dog took off, or he handed him off?"

"That's what I'm here to find out. I'm still getting a handle on what the legal situation is, but, from what I know at this moment, the government is very strict about the adopters of these dogs and has a contractual right to reclaim the dog if the proper owner is not with the War Dog. However, first I have to confirm that the dog is well cared for."

Rick nodded. "That could prove to be a bit of a problem."

"Why is that?"

"This guy doesn't let anybody get too close to the dog, but he does joke around a lot with the dog."

"Interesting, and what is he joking about?"

"It's an ongoing running joke," Rick noted, his voice low.

Julie's face pinched, as she leaned forward. "It's really nasty, what they keep talking about doing. Rick tells me to ignore it, and that it's just *men being men*," she shared, with a shrug. "But if that's men being men, I don't want any part of it."

"Exactly, but the dog should also be smart enough to get himself out of trouble, if he can," Rick pointed out. "We do have quite a few grizzlies up here. I don't know what is going on in this guy's head, but—"

"Do you like him?" Walton asked Rick, and, at his hesitation, Walton nodded. "You don't. ... That's good to know."

"It's not good to know," Rick countered, with a worried look. "They're paying guests, and that's what I care about."

"Not me," Julie snapped. "That's not the kind of paying guests we want, and it's certainly not what we want our lodge to be known for."

"No, of course not," Walton agreed, looking over at her. "So, we just have to ensure it doesn't mar your reputation."

"If it's not his dog, ... I would be more than happy for you to take it away," Julie stated, calming visibly.

"You don't like him either," Walton noted.

"No, I don't." She turned, then looked at Chelsea. "It'll be interesting to see if you do."

"If *you* don't, chances are I won't either," Chelsea replied.

Rick raised a hand, attracting their attention. "Hey, hey, hey, what's this? Women power? You at least could give the men a chance."

Chelsea looked over at him and shrugged. "Women are

fairly instinctive when it comes to these things. Thus, if Julie doesn't like him, chances are it's already decided."

"That's not fair," Rick pointed out.

"I don't really care," Chelsea muttered, then glanced around. "Didn't somebody offer me coffee?" She heard footsteps coming through the front door, with lots of raucous laughter.

The laughter stilled slightly as the group of four men came inside. The one who was clearly the head of the group studied the newcomers, nodded with a smirk, then turned his back on them. It was an acknowledgment and then a dismissal, also a chance for these men to adjust to the fact that they were no longer alone at the lodge.

"Right, we didn't rent the whole lodge, did we?" one of the men pointed out, causing more raucous laughter. "Glad to see some other people here." It was a very casual remark, yet he was clearly less than happy to have the company.

Smiling, Chelsea turned to him. "Hi, we'll be here for a few days. We enjoy the great outdoors at its best whenever we get the chance."

"So, you're not hunting?" asked one of the men.

She shook her head. "No thanks. I'm not into killing animals, if I don't need to."

"You like to eat them though, don't you?" he asked, his whole attitude needlessly aggressive.

"Absolutely," she replied, clearly unfazed. "I eat meat, but that doesn't mean I'm necessarily prepared to go out and shoot it myself. It's all about personal priorities."

"Of course," Walton agreed. This was a conflict he had come across many times over the years, and he understood both sides. If he needed to hunt for food for his survival, he could do it without a single qualm, but he also understood that it was not what Chelsea wanted to face right now. Wanting to change the tone in the room, he looked to Julie. "Did you say you had some coffee on?"

"Yep, it's over here." And she led the way to a sideboard that had a large pot of coffee sitting at the ready.

"Make sure you save some," one of the men called out. "I could really use a cup."

Chelsea smiled at him. "Not a problem."

"Yeah, the little women need to make the coffee while the men go out and hunt so they can eat," the same man added in a more belligerent tone.

Chelsea replied, "I'm a guest here too."

Walton watched as her back stiffened, and he looked over at Rick, who was probably wondering what kind of headache he had opened himself up to. He neared Rick and murmured, "This could be a fun few days."

Rick glanced at him sharply and whispered, "Let's hope so. It's a business for me."

"Understood." Walton turned to Chelsea, who was pouring coffee, yet her back remained noticeably rigid, a sure sign that she was more than irritated. "You may want to remind your sister of that."

Rick groaned. "*Yeah.* That horse is already out of the barn. When she's pissed off and worked up, it's beyond a lost cause."

Walton chuckled. "In that case, let the fireworks begin."

CHAPTER 3

CHELSEA ALREADY HATED him, Chad, the so-called leader of this group of hunters. It was hard to share the dinner table with these guys. This atmosphere surely didn't help her digest her food. Two others were almost as bad as Chad, with thankfully one guy just silent so far. However, Chad—who was sneering, commenting, and strutting around as if he owned the place—was a misogynistic asshole in his element up here, with no women around to rein him back in. He was just being the absolute epitome of a theoretical redneck, out in the middle of nowhere with guns and a bad attitude.

Everything that came out of his mouth was offensive, which just added fuel to the fire. Something inside her completely revolted in disgust, especially as she realized that Julie had probably been putting up with this crap from these guests.

When everyone was done eating, Chelsea helped Julie clean up, ignoring the jokes from the men behind them. They were jeering and chuckling, saying that at least Julie would have some help in the kitchen now that Chelsea was here. As she got into the kitchen, she spun around and glared at her sister-in-law. "Do you really put up with this crap all the time?"

Julie groaned. "I knew you wouldn't like that."

"No, of course not. Not when this is still your home."

"And it's our business," she pointed out.

"Are your guests all like this?"

"No, not at all," she hedged. "It's mostly this particular group. Something about them is even more raw-edged and angry than normal."

"*Raw-edged and angry*, really?"

Julie nodded.

"*Huh*. That's what the problem is, isn't it? They're really angry about something."

"I think they're angry about a few things," Julie noted. "I'm not quite sure what's going on, but today is the worst it's been."

"Because we arrived?" Chelsea asked.

"I don't know," she admitted, as she turned to Chelsea, then shrugged. "It's possible though."

"I'm really sorry about that because we didn't intend to make your life worse."

"Oh, gosh, you two being here is not worse," she replied, impulsively giving her a hug. "You're always welcome here. You know that."

"I might be welcome," Chelsea conceded, as a wave of displeasure racked her body, "but these guys? … They take the cake."

"They're definitely not my favorite guests," Julie shared, with a sigh. "So, it's something that we'll put down in our booking system, and they won't be welcomed back again. However, right now? … We can hardly kick them out."

"Really? I think it's time to establish some rules for these guests you have here."

"Normally we do, but this season has been pretty lean," Julie explained. "So, when they started acting like this, it wasn't the easiest to deal with, but we also need the money."

"Ah, crap." Chelsea rubbed her temples. "Is business that bad?"

"Let's just say it hasn't been very good."

"Of course not," she muttered. "Okay, fine. I'll try to get along."

Julie burst out laughing. "I would appreciate it, but I also know that, for you, it can be hard."

"I didn't think of myself as such a hothead, until I met that one guy."

"Yeah, Chad's the ringleader, the most obnoxious one of them all at that. Sometimes I think the other men are ready to apologize. Then Chad does something that stirs them up all over again."

"Yeah, because he wants them to be just as ugly and mean as he is."

Julie nodded. "Exactly. That's pretty much it."

"How long are they here for?"

"Supposedly another four days."

"That's interesting," Chelsea said. "What about the dog? It didn't come inside."

"No, he keeps it outside."

"Of course he does," Chelsea muttered. "You know that this War Dog element is likely to get ugly."

"I'm afraid it will," Julie conceded, looking at her. "I didn't want it to. Yet a part of me is really hoping something will happen, and they will leave."

"They might do just that," Chelsea noted, "because, if you think Walton will give up what he's been tasked to do, making sure the dog is okay—"

"Technically speaking, the dog is okay. Dog food is here, and I do ensure he's fed and has water, but it's not exactly a nice, comfy existence for him outside."

"The dog doesn't have to have luxury, but he does need to be well looked after. The dog put in how many years of service for our country, and then he ends up with an asshole?"

"This is life, and it happens."

"It happens, but it wasn't supposed to, and that's the thing Walton needs to figure out. What went wrong, and how does the War Department stop it from happening again?"

"I still can't believe anybody is here from the War Department, looking into a missing War Dog," Julie shared. "I mean, I figured most of the time that these animals are shipped off and shipped out, and nobody follows up."

"And that's what happened in this case. Nobody followed up, and it ended up being a problem because now nobody can find the man who was supposedly the one awarded custody of the dog."

"Interesting," she murmured. "Yet this guy doesn't talk about him at all."

"About the War Dog?"

"No, about the man who adopted the War Dog."

"That's interesting too. We'll see what happens because I'm warning you right now. Walton's got a bee in his bonnet about the dog and is definitely bothered about its well-being. I don't know why or what, but I know that when Walton was in the military, he worked a lot with K9 trainers—for all I know, maybe he's a trainer himself. But I do understand that these K9 dogs are very close to his heart."

At that, Julie just stared at her. "In other words, we won't get a good review, will we?" she muttered in a humorless tone.

Chelsea stared at her sister-in-law. "I'm not sure how to respond to that, but let's hope you don't need this review to stay in business," she pointed out.

"I won't let it be a problem," she muttered, "because these guys are not the kind of business we want around here."

"Good," Chelsea agreed, "because they seem to be a pretty rough-looking bunch."

"Oh, they are. Absolutely they are, and believe me that they don't give a crap about anybody else when they're all together."

"Has anybody approached you or done anything that really set off your alarm bells?"

"No," she replied, "but still I'm on alert. It's as if every day they are edging toward something. I just don't know what that something is."

"That's good to know." Chelsea stared at her.

"Yeah, it might be good to know, but it's also fairly unnerving because I feel as if something is seething under the surface. I don't know what it is, and I don't want to be around them to find out," she shared.

"So, do you need to stay?"

"I have to stay," she stated. "Nobody else is here to cook."

"I thought you had a cook at one time, didn't you?"

"We did, but she got COVID, and her father got COVID, and he ended up passing away. By then, given the state she was in, she decided to move south."

"Right, she was a fun lady, as I recall. Helen, was it?"

"Yeah, she was also our first guest."

"Do you still have the ability to call someone out, if need be?"

"Sure," Julie replied, "if need be, but not this time."

"Of course," Chelsea muttered. "Let's get dessert on the table, and we'll see how the evening goes from here. Let's hope it goes better."

"Yes, … and, Chelsea, stay close to Walton."

"Why is that?"

Julie hesitated. "People may be moving around in the night, and I don't want them to find out that you're in one room and that Walton is in the other. That'll leave them open to thinking you're available."

"I'm not available," she declared, frowning at her sister-in-law, "and even if I was—"

"I know. I know." Julie held up her hand. "It shouldn't be that way. I'm just telling you that something about these guys rings my bells, so it's best to stay out of their way."

"Got it," Chelsea conceded. "That's pretty unnerving though."

"Yeah, don't I know it. As far as I'm concerned, if you moved into Walton's room, I wouldn't be upset. As a matter of fact, I would welcome it just on the basis of your safety alone."

WALTON GOT UP the next morning and headed outside early. He'd gone out last night without telling anybody and made a quick check around the place to see just what he was up against. The War Dog had welcomed him with incredible happiness. The dog went by a different name now, with the new guy apparently calling him Brutus, which just aggravated Walton with its suggestion of aggression.

As he walked out in the early morning light, he stopped

by to see the War Dog looking lonely, out on the porch. He bent down and scratched his coat. "How're you doing, buddy?"

The dog welcomed him with an open heart, struggling to get up. "You've got a bad leg too, don't you?" Walton would have to check the file to confirm, but it was quite possible the War Dog was sidelined from duties not because of his age but because of an injury. Walton gently massaged the sore leg, as his own PT did for him, and the War Dog appeared to appreciate the attention.

When he heard movement inside, he got up and walked back into the lodge. Julie was putting on coffee. When she raised an eyebrow at him, he shrugged. "I'm an early riser."

"If I'd known that," she replied, "I would have shown you how to make the coffee."

He burst out laughing. "Show me now, and I'll do it tomorrow."

She nodded. "What were you doing outside?"

"Making friends with the dog."

She turned to him and asked, "Is it him?"

He nodded. "It is. Absolutely it is."

"How can you be so sure?"

"He's got the identifying tattoo on the inside of his leg."

"I guess I was hoping that it wasn't him and that we would get out of this relatively easily." When he looked at her, she shrugged. "Chad doesn't seem to be the kind of guy who will answer any questions easily."

"No, he sure doesn't, does he?" Walton agreed in a contemplative manner. "So, I guess we'll see what he says."

"They all got pretty drunk last night," she muttered. "For Rick, that's not cool, and not something he typically tolerates."

"It sounds as if they've been over the line in more ways than one. Yet Rick isn't doing anything about it. Are things that tight?"

"Honestly, yeah. These guys are paying a pretty hefty premium, so we need to keep them happy, as much as we can, for as long as we can."

"Sounds as if it's time for a review of your company policy."

"You're not kidding," she muttered, "and a way to dump these guys, if we could."

"And yet they haven't been like this the whole time?"

"No," she replied slowly, "but I can tell you that they've been getting worse and worse every day."

"Ah." Walton nodded. "That's a different story."

"Exactly, at least it is for me. They are really a difficult bunch, and I have a bad feeling about them," she shared. "I just need to get through the next few days, and then they're done here. Trust me when I say that they won't be welcomed back."

Walton grabbed a coffee and headed back outside again. As he played with the dog, a man snapped at him.

"It's not your fucking dog, so get the hell away."

Walton lifted his head and stared at the glaring man he'd come to recognize as Chad. Walton replied, "Nice dog. Is he yours?"

"Yeah, it's mine. Get the fuck away from it." Coming closer, he called the dog, and Brutus got up slowly and moved toward him.

"He's got quite the war injuries.," Walton noted.

"He's got injuries, but it's got nothing to do with war."

"Where did you find him?" Walton asked, watching as Chad continued to order the dog to come to him.

As soon as he got there, instead of petting him or praising him in some way, Chad glared back at Walton. "Doesn't matter. It's nothing to you."

"Not so sure about that. He's got an interesting tattoo."

"So what?"

"It's the tattoo of a War Dog."

Chad narrowed his gaze on Walton. "Still got nothing to do with you."

"That depends." Walton shook his head. "Where did you get him?"

Chad stiffened, jutted out his jaw, and declared, "Didn't you hear me? It's none of your fucking business."

"If it's not, it will be an interesting question for the War Department. What do you think?"

Chad froze. "What are you talking about?"

"The military keeps a long history on each of their War Dogs, including an exclusive adoption process. In order to adopt them," Walton explained, staring at the belligerent man, "there are certain requirements. I did record the War Dog's number, so I can double-check of course."

"What the hell? What are you talking about, *checking* it?"

"To see if *you* have the rights to this dog," Walton explained, "and I can tell from your attitude that you probably don't."

Chad jumped forward and got right in Walton's face.

Walton held his ground without flinching, knowing perfectly well that men like these thrived on inducing fear in their victims, just like bullies did elsewhere.

"I don't give a fuck what you say," Chad sneered, shoving his face even closer. "This is my dog, and you have no business fucking touching it."

"We'll see about that," Walton declared, "because one of the first things that every War Dog is entitled to is proper care and attention. So, rest assured. I'll be watching to see how you treat the dog over the next few days while I'm here," he pointed out. He kept his tone calm and even, though he was already certain that Chad had no rights to the dog. Now Walton had to figure out what the hell happened to the person who had adopted the dog in the first place. "So, here's the deal. If you can't tell me where you got the dog, I'll do a little research into your background."

Immediately Chad's eyebrows shot up. "What the fuck, man. I'm just here on a hunting trip."

"Yeah, but you're here on a hunting trip with a War Dog that you can't or won't explain possession of."

"That's just bullshit."

"Then tell me where you got him," Walton repeated.

"I don't need to explain anything to you."

"I will find out regardless, whether you tell me or not. It's just a matter of how much digging into your business I'll have to do." Chad didn't appear to know what to say. Still, if he lied on the adoption paperwork with the government, and it was proved to not be the truth, Chad could potentially be in trouble. Yet he didn't seem to give a crap if he was in trouble or not.

"I won't tell you jack shit," Chad snapped, with a sneer, "and absolutely no way you can make me. As for digging into my business"—he moved closer yet again—"you fucking damn well better not."

"Oh, you might be surprised what I do," Walton said, giving him a lazy smile. "You don't know anything about me."

"I know you walk with a fucking limp, so you're nothing

but half a man. I don't care what the hell happened or what you may be missing, but you can bet that I know exactly what you are. You're broken," he declared, with another sneer.

"Not as much as you may think," Walton pointed out. "And you better start facing reality when it's right in front of you."

"I would advise you to do the same. If it comes down to it, I'll beat you to a pulp without a care if you have any thoughts about causing me trouble."

"Is that because you've got enough trouble on your plate already, and you just can't handle more?"

"I can handle anything you throw at me," Chad snapped, glaring at him.

From inside the lodge, Julie called out, "Coffee is ready, gentlemen."

Chad snorted. "And, if you think these women will save your ass, you're wrong." Then he turned and stormed inside, but he left Brutus outside.

CHAPTER 4

CHELSEA WATCHED AS the men walked back inside. She glanced over at Julie to see her fingers clench and release, clench and release. Obviously whatever had gone on had stressed her out already. Chelsea walked over to Julie, and, grabbing her hand, pulled her a few steps away, and whispered. "Is everything okay?"

Julie shot her a look, gave a tremulous smile, and nodded. "It is. ... at the moment," she whispered, which spoke volumes about where this day was going.

Walking over to the coffeepot, Chelsea poured two cups of coffee, for her and Walton. One of the other men sneered at her. She raised an eyebrow. "Sorry, did you want something?"

"Yeah, a cup of coffee," he said.

She shrugged and pointed at the cups. "They're right there."

"Ah, aren't you a great little woman?"

She stiffened but tried hard not to let him see it. Turning away, she carried the two cups over to Walton, who separated himself and walked toward her.

One of the other men asked, "Wow, are you guys sticking around long? You're really putting a damper on our holiday."

"It's our holiday too," Chelsea noted, with a nod toward

Rick, who had just come in. "By the way, Rick's my brother."

At that, the men stiffened, looked at each other, then over at Rick. "She's your sister?"

Rick nodded. "She is."

"What the fuck, man."

"You've got a problem with that?" Rick asked.

"I sure do, especially pieces of shit family like this one." Chelsea rounded on him so fast that he backed up, hands out. "Okay, fine, that was uncalled for."

"You don't know me," she declared, staring at him, "and not only was that uncalled for, it didn't show a lick of common sense."

"I don't have to have common sense," he replied. "We've had a shitty couple of days. We were doing fine until you guys showed up."

"And you can leave anytime," Rick declared, his arms across his chest. "They have every right to be here, as much as you do."

"Yeah, well, we weren't expecting to share accommodations with people causing us trouble."

"I haven't caused you any trouble," Chelsea declared, wondering what had gotten their backs up.

"You and that shitty boyfriend of yours sure are."

"Why is that?" she asked.

"Digging his nose into our business, that's what," Chad stated, with a dirty look.

"Not everybody's," Walton clarified. "Just yours."

Chad stiffened at that, then turned to face him. "He's been running his mouth about me and Brutus," he explained, with a sneer.

"What about Brutus? He's your dog." One of his companions shot Walton a look and then turned back to Chad.

"How long has he had the dog?" Walton asked casually.

"About a week," the same guy replied.

"Longer than that," Chad corrected.

"No it wasn't. You sent photos of him a couple of nights before we arrived talking about it, but it wasn't all that long. I don't even think it's been one full week."

"It was a fucking couple weeks already," Chad snapped, glaring at his buddies.

One of them clammed up and shot a look at the others. "Okay, so it was a couple weeks. It's no big deal, and it's still his dog."

Walton shook his head. "That's a War Dog, and their histories and adoptions are heavily regulated by the War Department."

The guy just looked at Walton with a confused expression on his face. "And?" It was completely innocent, as if there was absolutely no way his buddy Chad could do anything wrong. Yet something else was in his tone that revealed he didn't have a clue whether his buddy had done something wrong or not.

Chad glared at Walton. "You keep your nose out of my damn business," he snapped. "I don't want to listen to any of this. We'll take a packed lunch out today," he declared, giving Julie an eyeful. "Better to be outside than to be anywhere around here right now."

Rick lifted an eyebrow. "You will be civil while you're here, or you're not staying. You are all guests here. It's just that simple. If you guys have problems with my sister visiting me while you're here, … that's on you. You keep it civil when on my property. Other guests and other people are here. And, by the way, you will be respectful to the women, or I'll kick you out myself." At that, he leveled his gaze at each and every one of the four men.

They all nodded, eventually even Chad. "That's fair, but she stays out of my way," Chad declared, looking scornfully at Chelsea.

"She doesn't have to stay out of your way," Rick replied. "She will be civil, as long as you are civil … or else."

The men just shrugged. Chad looked over at Julie and asked, "Can we get that packed-up lunch?"

"Of course." She turned and headed into the kitchen.

"I'll help," Chelsea offered and followed behind her.

At that, Chad snorted, "Or not."

She glared at him but didn't rise to the bait, walking away.

"I don't know what your problem is with my sister," Rick said, turning on Chad, "but that was uncalled for."

He shrugged. "She's with him, and I don't like him."

"I don't give a shit whether you like him or not. You are here on my property, and this is still my business. She's here, and she will stay here. She hasn't done anything to hurt you, and I've had enough of that crap from you. When you guys bring your asses back to the lodge today, adjust your attitudes beforehand."

Chad glared at him and then shrugged. "Maybe, but we need to go out and shoot off some steam."

"That's fine. Just ensure whatever you're shooting at is within your licensing."

"Ah, come on. … You won't be a stickler on that too, will you?"

"Absolutely I will," Rick declared. "I run a legit business here, and you knew that ahead of time."

Chad groaned. "Fine, we have tags, as you well know."

"Sure, and you're allowed to do what you want, *within reason*," Rick clarified. "Everything was fine yesterday. Don't make today a shit show."

"Too late." Chad glared at him. The men headed into the kitchen to get their to-go lunch.

Rick walked over to Walton. "You sure stirred up all kinds of shit on your first morning here."

He shrugged. "You also saw that Chad didn't have a clue what to say about the dog."

"I saw that," Rick noted, "so you better know your rights too. I won't say they're dangerous, but I have a hunch these guys could make your life pretty hellish."

"Yeah, just like a lot of other people in this world. These bullies pick on those they deem not as strong or as healthy as they are. I appreciate your requiring they treat the women right, but now that you've braced them, you'll have to watch your back yourself."

At that, Rick looked at him. "You think they're dangerous?"

"Yes, I do. Something is majorly off about Chad, and I don't like it. And let's not forget that they're all under suspicion of murder. That doesn't surprise me at all, now that I've met them."

Rick muttered, "Shit, I need this trip to go well. This is what I do, and my business depends on people having a great time, and, without it, I'm cooked. I was skeptical about their being trouble, until I saw their egos come out to play."

"I understand," Walton replied, "and I sure wasn't planning on bringing this kind of trouble here."

"I'm glad to hear that," Rick noted, "because, if I thought that you and my sister had done this on purpose, I would be pretty pissed."

"Honestly, I wasn't expecting such hostility," Walton muttered. "And the thing is, that started before I even mentioned the dog. On the other hand, knowing that they're here and that they're taking the dog out into the woods, I'm not so sure what my next move is. Do you know where they're going?"

Rick nodded. "Yeah, generally. I have some routine areas."

"Are you going out as their guide?"

"Not this time. I showed them a couple places to set up in blinds. Why?"

"If you want to show me, I think I'll head out and see what they're up to."

"Oh, Jesus, I wouldn't do that," Rick said in alarm. "I don't trust them at all at this point."

"Maybe not, yet I also need to know what's going on with the dog."

"You must really like this person who asked you to help out because I feel as if you're heading into dangerous territory."

"I am, and I do, but, most of all, that War Dog, and others like him, need a chance to relax and rest, not go out and be pitted against bigger animals for some assholes' sick entertainment."

"They keep joking about it, but I don't know that it's serious," Rick shared. "I mean, guys like Chad shoot the shit all the time when they're up here."

"Of course they do," Walton conceded. "I get that, but I need to keep tabs on what they're up to."

"Yeah, and what if they see you? If these guys get a few drinks under their belts, … they're a whole different breed, particularly when they've got weapons on them."

"So, they'll be drinking out there too?" Walton asked, frowning at Rick.

"They're not supposed to, but it wouldn't be the first time I've had somebody try it, and these guys would be just the type to do it. If it's target practice, it's one thing, and I tend to let it slide." Rick shrugged. "Yet it's something else entirely if they're hunting. That's a whole different story altogether."

Walton didn't say anything more, as Rick turned to watch the men as they packed up and headed out. Walton was still nursing the same coffee that Chelsea had brought him, and she now stood at his side. "I thought you were helping Julie."

"She told me to get out of the kitchen." Chelsea wrinkled up her nose. "I figured, given the sudden unpleasantness, that maybe I should do as she asked and stay out of the way."

"Much appreciated," Rick noted at her side.

"I'm sorry. I didn't have any clue this would be the way things went down."

"That's good because I would kick your ass into tomorrow myself if I thought you did it on purpose."

With a bunch of loud bangs of the front doors closing, the men finally exited the lodge. Silence fell. Walton walked over to the window and watched as the men headed out. "They're just walking from here?"

Rick nodded. "A ridge is not too far that's got great sites for hunting." Walton just nodded, his gaze checking out the area. "You'll really go after them, won't you?" Rick asked.

Walton nodded again, without saying anything.

"You're what?" Chelsea cried out.

He turned to her. "I just want to get an idea of what

these men are like when they're out on their own."

"What they are is likely to shoot you in the back if they see you," Chelsea exclaimed.

"That's one of the reasons I want to go," Walton confirmed.

"You want to go, so you can get shot?" she asked, staring at him in shock.

"No, I want to go so I can see if that's really what we're up against. Don't forget that these men are suspected of a murder and, on top of that, the murder of one of their own friends," he pointed out. "They operate a bit like a gang, and they're all up here because they had a tough time with a bunch of interrogations."

"I wonder why," she quipped, staring at him. "You do realize that's it's suicide for you to go out there, especially when they've already shown how much hate they have for you."

"We need to know if they are getting to the point of shooting somebody in cold blood. If they are those kinds of men, there's a good chance that they're guilty in that criminal case down in Mississippi, and that's something I've got to find out."

Rick added, "It won't matter if they are or not, if you're not alive to provide any evidence. You'll be dead, and it won't make a damn bit of difference." Rick spat out some chew on the ground now that they were all standing outside, looking in the direction the men had gone.

"Maybe," Walton conceded, with a shrug. "I don't think they'll be quite that bad. They are just blow-hard bullies when other people are around. However, I'm not so sure about that Chad dude."

"He's the worse of the lot," Chelsea noted. "He just incites everybody into something so much uglier."

"That's how he feels powerful. He can make people do what he wants," Walton pointed out.

"But why would they allow that?" Chelsea asked.

"Chad rules by fear," Walton explained. "Whatever is going on here, did you see any signs of real friendship between them? I didn't. I saw fear and plenty of it. Chad's holding something over them, and they're all here because *Chad* wanted to go on a hunting trip. They're not here because they wanted to come kill things. They're here because he ordered them to be here. Now the question is why, and what do we need to know about it?"

"How about nothing," Chelsea suggested. "It has nothing to do with the dog."

"I don't know about that," Walton countered, staring at her. "At the moment, I'm not sure that we can rule out anything."

"Maybe not, but we also don't know what the hell's going on here, and you're going out there after them. That won't help."

"I'm here to look after the dog," Walton declared, "and that's the job I will do."

"And, if it gets you killed, do you think Kat wants that?"

"No, she doesn't," he agreed, "but she wouldn't have asked me to do this if she didn't think I could handle it."

"What the hell does she know about what shape you're in?" Rick asked from the sidelines.

"She knows better than anybody," Walton replied. "She's the one who designs and manufactures my prosthetics."

"Jesus." Chelsea scrubbed her face. "I also know that you're not fully healed, and, if you go out there hiking, following the trail where those men have gone, that's bound to be pretty rough terrain."

"And they'll end up overlooking a ridge, which won't be the same thing as them tracking me down," Walton pointed out. "Remember that this is the kind of work I always did."

"What? Secret missions?" she teased.

He smiled at her and nodded. "Exactly."

WALTON DIDN'T TAKE a weapon with him. Some were at Rick's place, but, if something bad were to happen, Walton didn't want Rick interrogated over why he gave Walton a weapon. Instead he asked Julie about filling a thermos for him. "I'm just going out for a walk." He knew it wouldn't make them any happier. He smiled to see the look of concern on Chelsea's face. Rick and Julie were also giving him that same look. "You're welcome to come for a walk if you want, Chelsea," he offered. "It will blunt any theories of my following them and lend credence to my being out there, if they see us together."

"Except that they don't think much of my sister either," Rick warned. "You won't learn much about what they're up to if they know you're out there."

Chelsea turned on her brother. "It does make sense though. It gives Walton some cover as to why he is out there. We would be just another couple, enjoying our trip."

"What?" Rick asked them. "So, you'll exacerbate the problem by going out at the same time?"

"But he's right," Chelsea noted. "It will provide something of an excuse. Besides, what else can he do to confirm the dog is okay?"

Rick shook his head. "They've got the War Dog out there. If Chad's not allowed to keep it, just call the authorities and have them take it back again."

"That's what I'm here for. I will take possession of the dog, once I get some info back. I've got several inquiries into what's going on with the original adopter," Walton explained, "but I've heard nothing so far."

"Which means you can't do anything at the moment?" Chelsea asked.

"I can't reclaim the dog yet, but that doesn't mean I shouldn't continue to collect my own information. Eventually I will have to act on behalf of the War Department."

"What did you think of the condition of the dog?" Rick asked.

"He was good," Walton noted, waving his hand. "Looks as if he's had an injury, and that may well be why he was retired. But now Chad's got me very curious as to how long he's had the War Dog and what happened to the original owner."

"You don't think Chad did something to the legal owner, do you?" Chelsea asked.

"I hope not," Walton replied, "but you saw Chad. Aggressive, ill-mannered, quick to fire, quick to get ugly, zero patience, zero control. … He could easily had been involved in the murder of his friend, so I do worry about the War Dog's lawful owner."

"Sure, but the death of their friend won't be your problem, will it?" Chelsea asked, frowning.

"Not necessarily"—he smiled in her direction—"only if I make it so."

"You've been talking to the Mississippi cops too, haven't you?" Julie asked.

"Of course I have," he confirmed, with a laugh. "It's not in me to just watch Chad and his buddies out here, acting as they are, without checking up on them."

"And you do know that's sticking your nose into other people's business?" Chelsea noted.

"Yep, I know," he agreed. "It never goes well for some people."

"No, it really doesn't," Chelsea declared, stomping her foot.

He smiled at her. "Wow, look at that—a temper."

"Oh, she's got a temper all right," Rick stated, chuckling. "We used to call her Debby Dragon because she was such a spitfire."

"And yet her name isn't even Debby," Walton noted.

"No, it isn't. All the more of a shame." Rick chuckled. "Look. I'm okay with your going out there, even the two of you just going for a walk, but you know that any confrontation with these guys will end up ugly."

"I know," Walton said, "but at least then it wouldn't be happening here at your lodge. It is a win-win situation for you nonetheless."

"Yet they will return to my lodge. Plus, they're still on my property," Rick pointed out. "So that argument doesn't really work for me."

"I'll try not to get into any arguments with them. How's that?"

"Good enough," Rick muttered.

Julie walked out just then with a thermos. She handed it to them and added, "Please be careful."

"Will do," Walton replied. "We'll just walk up in the direction where they are, confirm they are there, so that we know for sure. I'll listen in a bit to their private conversations. Then Chelsea and I will walk in the opposite direction and maybe do a bit of a hike."

"Oh, I like the sound of that better," Chelsea shared, turning to face Walton. "We won't just sit here and surveil them, right?"

"Nope, we sure won't. In the meantime, I'm waiting for information from Kat and her husband."

And, with that, they quickly packed up, put on the hiking boots they had brought, plus their heavy coats, and, with a final check on the weather, they headed out, following the same route as the hunters.

When they got out of sight of her brother, Chelsea looped her arm through Walton's and asked, "What are you not telling me?"

He frowned at her. "What do you mean?"

"It definitely feels as if you're hiding something."

"If I am, I don't really understand what it would be," he said. "Look. I have suspicions and all kinds of thoughts about what's going on here, but I don't have any insider knowledge yet."

As they walked, his phone buzzed. He looked down at the text on his screen and smiled. "Now this gives us another reason to be extra careful, but also another reason to check up on the dog."

"Why is that?"

"The owner's in the hospital. He was beaten up at his house one night. His caregiver stopped by the next day and found him on the floor, and the War Dog was gone. They rushed him to the hospital, and he's been there ever since."

"Well, shit." She came to a dead stop. "You think it was Chad?"

"It's a definite possibility," he agreed, with a nod. "He's

certainly got the temper for it."

"Oh, Christ," she muttered. "What kind of man is Chad?"

"One who's up on suspicion of murder, remember?"

She winced. "I don't really want to even think about that."

"Of course not." He chuckled. "Still, we need to be aware that Chad could be dangerous as hell. If he hurt that old man in order to get the War Dog from him, then Chad has no scruples, and that will show up very quickly when we're dealing with him."

"It's already showing," she noted. "Honestly, just being close to you makes me feel safer, even though we're out here. Chad turned on me pretty damn fast back there."

"I'm glad Rick put him in place, but I don't know that it will be enough."

"I have my doubts too," she agreed. "Chad just seems to be angry about so much."

"Of course, and whether he was behind the killing of his friend or one of his other friends did it, Chad feels as if he's caught in the middle. … So it's still an ugly place to be."

"You really think one of these guys killed their own friend?"

"When you think about it, this bunch of guys were the only ones nearby. I think the problem the police are having is that they don't know which one did it or if all of them are involved."

"So, a conspiracy then?"

"I don't know that it's a conspiracy," he hedged, with a smile. "The thing to remember is that just because somebody told the cops something, it's still a mess to really find out the truth."

They walked along in the early morning light, content to just be outside.

"Is this really the time that most people hunt?" she asked.

It wasn't necessarily the right time for hunting, and he was surprised the hunters had gone out at this hour. "It depends on whether they're planning to sit in a blind all day or just getting out and wandering around," he shared.

"I don't think I would like hunting much anyway, but sitting in a blind all day sounds terrible."

"There are different ways to hunt, and, for a lot of people, sitting in a blind is perfect." He smiled at her. "Everybody has their preferences, and some are very particular about the way they go about it."

"Of course," she muttered, "especially these guys."

As it was, where the men were planning on hunting wasn't very far ahead. They heard them well before they got there.

She muttered to Walton, "Do they really expect to hunt something when they're talking so loud?"

He placed a finger against her lips and pulled her off to the side, whispering against her ear, "It sounds as if they're arguing, and I want to get close enough to hear what they're saying."

She looked up at him and then nodded. "Do you want me to stay here?"

A ghost of a smile sneaked out, and he nodded. "Yeah, kind of. I can get there pretty quietly if I'm traveling alone."

"Even with your leg?"

He frowned as he looked down at it and nodded. "Yes, even with my leg." And, with that, he tucked her up behind one of the many trees and told her, "I'll be back in twenty."

"And what if you're not?"

"If I'm not, you head back to your brother." She frowned, clearly not understanding. "If I'm not back by then, I'm probably not able to get back at all."

Her eyes widened in shock, but he quickly disappeared, not giving her too much time to argue with him. She wasn't great at following orders to begin with, and this would likely be a request she really struggled with. As it was, Walton had only gotten another ten or twenty feet away, still in sight of each other, when they heard crashing through the woods and more yelling.

"Jesus fucking Christ. I can't believe you made us come up here, Chad. You know we don't like hunting."

"I don't give a shit what you like," Chad bellowed. "I know one of you fucking assholes killed Rudy, and I want to know which one of you did it. This was a great cover to get us all out here, in the middle of nowhere, so we can talk, and so nobody can hear us."

"Really? You think one of us killed Rudy? And yet you brought that stupid dog. Where the hell did you get it anyway?"

"Doesn't matter where I got it. It's mine," he declared, his tone defiant.

"Not if the guy back there has any say about it."

"I don't give a shit what he says," Chad muttered. "And just to be clear. I don't really give a shit what you say either. Yet, if you fucking killed Rudy, I'll pop you too."

"Oh, for Christ's sake, Chad. None of us killed him."

Walton thought Darren was speaking to Chad, but it might have been Hawk.

"The cops seem to think *I* killed him," Chad noted.

"What the hell? … You say the cops are looking at you,

but I thought you did it too," Darren quipped, with a laugh. "Are you telling us that you didn't?"

"No, I didn't," Chad declared, "but, if you did, … that was a shit move. Rudy had a wife and kids."

"Like you give a fuck about wives and kids, man. Every time you even see a woman, you practically go off on her, screaming and hollering that she's toxic to the world, some poison to be wiped out."

"They're all fucking poison," Chad snapped.

"Because your wife left you? … Jesus Christ, Chad. They're not all that way."

"The hell they aren't," Chad argued. "You just don't believe it."

"No, I don't believe it. No reason to be treating them as you are. It just makes you look damn suspicious."

At that came dead silence. "Suspicious of what?" Chad snapped, as he stormed closer to his supposed buddy.

Walton slipped around a tree and climbed up so that he could see, at least getting a visual of who was arguing with whom. As he stopped in the tree about midway up, he caught just part of the scene, although not all of it. He quickly jumped up to the branch above his head and climbed up another level. Peering through the branches, he had a much better view.

The four men were squared off against each other, dispelling all thoughts about being on a hunting trip. The trouble was, they were all more or less in a circle, and it was damn hard to see who was speaking because Walton couldn't keep his eye on all of them at the same time.

"I'm not saying you did anything, Chad," Hawk replied in exasperation, "but, Jesus Christ, knock it off, will you?"

Darren added, "Nobody killed Rudy. It was an accident."

"Maybe it was an accident," Chad conceded, "but I still think it was one of you guys."

"Then why did the cops think it was you?" Darren asked, staring at him.

"They had some insider tip, and that's just bullshit because I didn't do it."

"That's fucking fantastic, man," Hawk said. "If you didn't do it, you've got nothing to worry about."

"That's bullshit, and you know it," Chad argued. "The minute the cops get their eyes on you, it's pretty hard to shake them off."

In a sad way, Walton understood that because sometimes it was hard to shake off the authorities long enough to even consider looking in another direction when trying to find the real criminal. Still, that didn't mean this Chad guy was innocent. Yet it sounded as if Chad himself may not have done anything, and that was too bad because Walton would be quite happy to lock that guy up. And, with this group, there was still the possibility that they had a murderer among them.

Chad had such a shitty attitude on life and women that the poor War Dog would have a hell of a life with him, unless Walton could get Brutus free of this man. Walton wanted to know what really happened with the valid owner too.

"Another thing," Hawk added, "what the hell is the deal with that damn dog? You didn't have the dog even a week ago, so why are you so defensive, and why is the guy back there all over you about it?"

"Shit, man," Darren noted, "if you stole the dog just a week ago, and this guy came down on you this quick, I can only imagine what's happening behind the scenes."

Walton witnessed Chad starting to sweat.

"It ain't nothing," Chad muttered. "I won him in a bet, that's all."

Hawk shared, "I don't think this guy will think very highly of that because winning a goddamn War Dog in a bet doesn't mean the transaction was scrutinized to a tee. Besides, you already have a criminal record, so the government or the military would probably never even let you have a damn War Dog for real."

"What does that even mean?" Darren asked. "Christ, he is a broken-down dog, not a War Dog."

Chad groaned. "That's because the dog came from an overseas war where he did time, like that piece of shit guy who's poking into our business. We should just pop him and put him to rest," Chad suggested, venom in his tone.

"Would you stop going around telling everybody you'll pop them?" Hawk glared at Chad. "It just makes us sound like murderers, and I didn't have anything to do with Rudy's death."

"Neither did I," added George, the fourth man in the group, who mostly remained quiet.

"Then what happened to Rudy?" Chad asked suspiciously. "He was right there with all of us, then suddenly he was dead."

"You tell me." Hawk glared at him. "You were the last one to see him."

"No, I wasn't." Chad turned and pointed to Darren. "What about you?"

"What about me? I was with you," he said begrudgingly. "You've been going off half-cocked over this ever since."

"Yeah, because the cops are breathing down my neck. I

did time once, and they're always looking at a fucking criminal as if we have nothing better to do than go out and cause more hell."

"Maybe that's what they're thinking, and it's *because* of your criminal record," Darren pointed out, "but that doesn't mean that *we* did anything to make it happen."

Chad asked, "So why can I easily imagine one of you guys pointing a finger at me? With the way it happened and the way the cops are on me, it makes my life miserable. Jesus Christ, what the hell are we even doing here?"

"I thought we were coming out to have a nice visit together," George replied.

"No, you didn't." Hawk turned, shaking his head at George. "That's complete bullshit," Hawk declared. "You know damn well you came up here out of curiosity, George, trying to figure out what the hell is going on."

"That's true. I did." George laughed.

But the high note to that laugh made Walton sit up straight and listen.

Hawk added, "You're all just going off half-cocked. What did you do, Chad? Beat up some guy to get the damn dog? If so, you're nuts. That's the kind of stunt that'll get your ass pulled into jail," he muttered, as he looked first at the dog and then back over at Chad. "Whether you did anything to Rudy or not, I don't know, but, Christ, Chad, did you really steal a War Dog?" Hawk asked, on a roll now. "They are chipped, you know? There's a paper trail as to ownership, and it ain't easy to be approved to have one. These fucking War Dogs are locked down like you wouldn't believe."

"I did try to get one," Chad muttered, "and they denied me."

"Ever wonder why?" Hawk asked. "You're probably not stable enough for one. Not to mention your criminal record. That's part of what the military does, you know? They try to find out who is stable enough to handle one of these dogs and who'll treat it right. Christ, I wouldn't give you one either."

"What the fuck are you talking about?" roared Chad, as he charged Hawk.

Hawk laughed, did a quick sidestep, then tripped Chad and dropped him. "I've told you before, Chad. Don't even fucking come at me like that. I came up here to see what the hell was going on and which one of you popped Rudy and what we would do about it. Because if anybody comes after me with any accusation, you can sure as hell bet that I'm not taking the fall."

"I didn't fucking shoot Rudy," Chad grumbled.

"Neither did I," Hawk said.

"Neither did I," Darren added.

"And neither did I," George stated.

All four men stared at each other.

"If it wasn't us, who was it then?" George asked. "The cops are looking at us as being the only suspects, and they're following us every damn place we go, and that sucks. I don't really want the cops on my ass all the time. We came up here to solve this, so let's solve it."

"How will you do that?" Chad asked, as he sat cross-legged on the forest floor, staring up at him in disgust. "You think we haven't tried? What is it you want to do? It's not as if we have any answers here."

"One thing's for sure. … If somebody here did it, they're trying to hide it," Hawk suggested. "So everybody work out where you were, and maybe, if we figure out who it was, which one of us did it, at least we know who we can throw the book at, when we get back home again."

"So, hang on a minute. You want to figure out which one of us killed Rudy, and then you'll turn someone in?" Chad asked, his tone rising in anger. "What kind of friendship is that?"

"I'm not a friend of any asshole who pops one of our friends," George interrupted in that same lazy tone. He seemed to be not so much a leader but the one who steps to the side, his gaze strong and watchful, as he studied the rest of them. "If you guys think that killing our friend and then going on a trip is okay, I'm telling you that something is wrong with all of you."

"I agree with that," Darren replied. "What the hell are we even doing here?"

Hawk shook his head. "That was not my question at all. I want to know what we'll do to get out of this mess with the cops."

"I sure as hell don't want to shoot a deer in order to prove that we're here," George muttered.

"Oh, fuck off. You might not want the meat, but I do," Chad declared. "So, if we're out here hunting, the least we can do is make good on it."

"Why?" Darren asked. "I don't particularly even like deer meat." One of the other men laughed, but Walton couldn't see who it was.

"That's just great," Hawk muttered. "Here we are on a hunting trip. A couple of us don't even like to hunt and don't even like to eat deer meat. This is some sort of mockery."

"It was a chance to sort ourselves out," Chad stated defiantly, "and each of you came willingly enough."

"I'll admit I came," Hawk shared. "I don't know about how *willing* I was since you threatened me, told me that you had something on me and that, if I didn't come, you would tell my wife."

At that, George laughed and looked over at Chad. "What the fuck, man? You can't blackmail friends like that."

"I wanted to know what he was up to, and I didn't know if he's the one who threw me to the wolves about Rudy," Chad replied. "So I had to make him come. How else would I get him here?"

"You did the same thing to me, threatening to tell my boss whatever you think you know," Darren stated, "and I sure as fuck don't appreciate it. Now we're all here, and somebody shot Rudy, and you set up a hunting trip so we're all carrying weapons? What the hell, man? I didn't come up here to die."

"I didn't either," Chad snapped, staring at him, "but I sure as hell didn't come up here to have the cops thrown my way either."

"The cops already came your way, before this trip," Hawk pointed out, "and nobody here had to do anything. You've got a criminal record, and that automatically made you the number one suspect."

"Maybe, but I didn't do it," Chad declared. "So whichever one of you guys did pop Rudy, you need to fess up, so I can get cleared."

"Hang on a minute," Darren said. "So now you want us to fess up as to who killed Rudy and then what? You'll take us back on a citizen's arrest?"

"Maybe," Chad said, with a glare. "That's better than my going to fucking jail for the rest of my life for something I didn't do. It's one thing if I did do something, but it's another thing entirely if I didn't, which I did not," he snapped.

Just then the branch that Walton sat on snapped, tumbling him to the ground. Swearing under his breath, he quickly ducked into the brush off to the side, but already the four men raced in his direction.

"What the fuck was that?" Darren asked.

"I bet you it's that fucking dog lover," Chad swore. "What if he fucking heard us?"

"We didn't say anything," Darren noted. "I mean, if we didn't kill anybody, we didn't kill anybody. So, it's no fucking big deal."

"It is a big deal if we did kill somebody," Chad noted, looking from one to the other. "That's the thing. Did one of us kill him, or was it somebody else?"

"If it was somebody else, who the hell was it?" Hawk asked.

"Did you ever think that maybe Rudy offed himself?" Darren asked in a wary tone. "I've been over and over and over this. If none of us killed him, maybe Rudy did it to himself."

They all sat very quietly at the same spot where Walton had just dropped. He was barely ten feet from them, and he desperately needed to send a message to Chelsea to let her know that they were coming her way. Hopefully she had the smarts to stay hidden if the men did come in her direction because these guys were already upset and angry. If they saw her, there was no guarantee what they would do.

One thing Walton would never do was trust men who were drinking, angry, armed, and afraid. Primal fear was at the base of Chad's anger. He was afraid that he would get slammed for something he hadn't done. But, if he didn't kill

Rudy, who the hell did, and how would this all play out?

Another question popped into Walton's mind, and that was a possibility too. Had somebody pinned the murder on Chad?

He made a great patsy. Walton would have done it himself if there was any reason to. The man obviously had some big temper issues and a chip on his shoulder to boot, but still, if Chad didn't kill their friend Rudy, somebody else did, and Walton would still bet it was somebody in this group. The question was, who did it?

CHAPTER 5

CHELSEA HEARD THE men approaching and swore under her breath. She hunkered down lower and deeper into the brush at the base of the tree line, hoping they wouldn't see her. She couldn't imagine what would happen if they did. She didn't want to meet them in the dark, and she had no clue what the hell their problem was, other than a severe hatred of women. She figured it would probably be because of divorces or something along that line, but these men were a little too angry and adamant about women for her liking. It's almost as if they were in a dedicated women-haters club.

"What the fuck, man? What are you bringing up your wife for?" Chad asked Hawk, as they walked onward. "You know that's a taboo subject for us. Christ, you're the only one who's even still married."

"Yeah, and I want to keep it that way."

"Why?" Chad snapped. "She's fucking ugly."

"Hey, hey, hey, you want to keep things civil around here? Then you stop insulting my wife," he snapped.

One of the other men laughed.

Hawk noted, "Back in the day none of us had wives, or, if we did, we didn't like them, and that was what started this lovely little gang to begin with. We were the wife-haters club, the women-are-bitches club," he shared, with a laugh. "Then slowly over time, more and more stepped out of that."

"Just you," Darren noted.

"No, not just me, *Darren*. Maybe you guys haven't even heard, but Darren here is engaged."

Everybody froze, and Chelsea could still see them right at the edge of her vision. She held her breath, waiting, wishing they would just get moving.

Chad gave Darren a hard smack on the shoulder. "What the fuck, man?" Chad muttered.

"What?" Darren asked. "I'm in love. I want to get married, and it's none of your fucking business."

"What the hell are you even here for?" Chad asked.

"I don't know," Darren cried out. "I have no clue, and you guys are fucking nuts. What started out as half a joke and a need to just get out and vent because we were unhappy has now turned into some poisonous little group. Just look at the way you talked to that poor woman today, Chad, even the woman from the lodge. Jesus, Rick's wife, Julie, she's a sweetheart, and you treat her like shit."

"I never treated her like shit. It's the other bitch who I treated like shit. Come on. We all agreed that nobody would get married again."

"Sure, we all agreed to that when we were all hurting and hating," Hawk admitted, as he walked forward, "but life doesn't stay stagnant, Chad. You move on, or at least you hope you move on, because, Jesus Christ, you guys, this is sad. Listen to you all. You're just pathetic."

Darren snapped, "Two of us now have partners. Surely we don't need to all be part of the same old women-hating group anymore."

"What? So, you want to disband the group?" Chad asked.

"Christ, you know Rudy was looking at getting married again, right?" Darren asked, a hurting note in his tone.

"What, Rudy was divorcing his wife, the mother of his kids?" Hawk asked.

Darren nodded. "Yeah, Rudy was because he really cared about somebody else."

"Maybe his current wife fucking popped him one," Chad snapped.

Chelsea could barely see, but now she heard footsteps thumping on the ground as the men headed back to the lodge. She didn't know what was going on, but, man, that conversation was something else. Just when she thought they had passed, and she was safe, a cold wet nose slipped into her hand, making her jump, which completely blew her cover.

WALTON HEARD THE rustle too.

The four men froze. "What the hell was that?" Chad asked.

Hawk nodded. "I heard something. It sounded human."

"I don't know about human, but a lot of birds out here talk," George noted.

More muffled sounds came, and then there was a bark.

Walton swore, realizing that Brutus had effectively found Chelsea. It was also the kind of work that Brutus used to do, and it was a good thing on his part, but really shitty timing here. Walton should have considered that. Swearing softly, he heard the men speaking again.

"Stop being such a baby," Chad ordered.

"He's right, man," Darren snapped. "All kinds of animals are out here. Just because we've got guns doesn't mean that we're prepared for any attacks."

"Let's just go back and grab some lunch," Hawk added.

"We've got a take-out lunch, for Christ's sake. Remember that we're supposed to be out hunting?" Chad sneered. "You guys are no more fucking hunters than that other duo up there."

"No, maybe not, and maybe he's an undercover cop, looking to see if you really did kill somebody." George sneered. "I wouldn't be at all surprised."

A dead silence came that quickly turned very ugly. "Do you think he is?" Chad asked.

"I don't fucking know, and I don't care," George replied. "I haven't done anything wrong, and, if you haven't either, then leave it already."

"I didn't say I hadn't done anything wrong. I just said I didn't kill him. I didn't kill Rudy."

Hearing the conversation, Walton moved as quickly as he could back to Chelsea, when all of a sudden there was another bark.

Hawk said, "Get the goddamn dog back here, will you?"

With that, Chad whistled several times. "Come on, Brutus. Get over here. No fun and games for you today. God, these guys are such fucking spoilsports."

When they saw no sign of Brutus, the men just trudged toward the hunting lodge. "He'll come. Don't worry," Chad muttered.

Darren added, "Maybe it would be better if he didn't, ... considering he's not even your fucking dog."

At that came more ugly silence. "Let's get one thing straight," Chad snapped, and he sounded mad. "That is my dog, and, if you say anything else about it, we'll have a problem."

"I have no problem with it," Hawk shared, "but why are you so defensive and ugly about it?"

"Because I don't like you fucking trying to get me in trouble, and it's my dog."

As they walked on ahead, Walton just barely kept them in front of him, but it was hard to keep track of the conversation now. Then Walton sensed an absolutely silent movement, just a slip of a motion beside him. He turned, and there was Brutus. Walton grinned, squatted, and opened his arms. Brutus flung himself into them and gave Walton a raucous welcome. The rustling in the bush may have been responsible for the sudden silence of the men, which then had them speeding up their footsteps as they raced away.

"Good boy," Walton murmured to Brutus, "good boy." Hearing something else, he turned to see Chelsea straighten up ever-so-slightly. He smiled. "You can come over here and say hi."

She raced to his side. "He shoved his nose into my hand," she whispered, as she bent down to cuddle Brutus. "Startled me, and I was scared he would let them know I was here."

"I was a little worried for your sake too," he admitted. "Another reason you should stay home next time."

"Yet I didn't want to," she said, with spirit, glaring at him.

"I knew that," he agreed, with a nod, "but how about now?"

"We don't want to come in right behind them, so I suggest we skirt around. A lake is about one mile away on the other side over here," she shared.

"How do you know? Had you been there before?"

"Yes, but I'd forgotten. Julie told me, if we got tired of

their fighting, that the water feature was off to the side, but the opposite direction of where we went, and that's when I remembered it."

He paused, looked around, and then nodded. "Might not be a bad idea. We don't want those guys to think that we're out here following them."

"Which we were," she admitted, with a shrug, "so it would make sense if they thought that."

"Maybe, but we don't want to confirm that," he pointed out.

And, with Brutus at their side, who appeared to have no intention of leaving them alone, Walton turned them to the right, even as she started to go off a different way. He shook his head.

"What?" she asked in exasperation, her hands on her hips.

"Wrong direction," he noted, with a gentle smile. Then he pointed. "The hunting lodge is there."

She frowned and shrugged. "I'll trust you on this one, but if you're wrong …"

"I know," he replied, with a grin. "If I'm wrong, I'm the one who's in trouble."

She laughed. "I don't imagine *trouble* is quite the right word, but the sooner we're away from whatever direction those guys were traveling, the better."

And, with that settled, they picked up the pace and moved rapidly toward the lake. She looked down at Brutus. "What about him?"

"What about him?" Walton asked in the same tone.

"I don't like the idea of Chad thinking the dog disobeyed him."

"Brutus did disobey Chad, and that's a concern because

obviously Brutus would rather be with us than with Chad. That tells us how the War Dog feels about Chad."

"He also was pretty adamant that the dog is his."

"Yeah, and I am also adamant about checking out the police report on the man who was beaten up and lost the dog," Walton shared, "because I'm starting to get a pretty good idea who did it."

"Jesus, would Chad really do that?"

"What do you think?"

"Yeah, you don't even need to ask me again," she muttered. "Chad absolutely would do that. He's just that kind of belligerent asshole."

"Let me send a text, if we have any cell service among this tree cover. If not, at least I can get it written up." As they walked, their pace a little slower, he quickly texted the detective he'd spoken with earlier. With that *Sending* but not yet sent, he smiled at her. "At least now we have a better idea of what's going on."

"No, we don't," she countered, frowning at him. "Every one of them is saying they didn't have anything to do with the killing of their friend, and they're all basically saying the dog isn't Chad's."

"That's because the dog isn't his, but, for whatever reason, he ended up with it. Whether he beat up the guy himself, or during the beating he decided to take the dog, I don't know. However, we can obviously see that the dog doesn't obey him and doesn't know him, outside of maybe Chad being the one who brought Brutus here. Dogs have particular loyalties, and, if Brutus has an owner to go back to, you can bet Brutus will want to return to him."

"But only if he was well treated there too."

"Exactly, but I don't have any reason to believe that the

man who was beaten up abused the dog. Brutus is a beautiful dog, in good shape but slightly handicapped by his past injuries. Brutus would have been able to relate to his retired veteran owner on so many levels."

"Right, Brutus is not currently injured though, right? It's not as if these guys have hurt him any more than he already was, correct?"

"No, I don't believe so," Walton replied, with a nod, "and that's a very distinctive point because I don't think they've beaten him up any more than he may have already been beaten up in terms of life and war in general."

She smiled. "That is something you should recognize."

He shrugged. "To a certain extent, yes, but, other than that, it's just life. I got beaten up too, but I'm still here and still kicking."

She chuckled. "I would think so, and you're doing a mighty fine job of it."

He shrugged. "I don't know about that, but I am still kicking, and you know more about my condition than I do."

"I know that you're still working at it," she shared, "although you canceled our last appointment. Why is that?"

He nodded and then squared his shoulders, and she felt his guard going up. "I did. I wasn't feeling so great." When she raised an eyebrow, he shrugged. "I ended up getting more surgery and needed to lay low, to recover a bit."

"But then," she added, "you used it as an excuse to not come back in again."

He grinned at her. "What's the matter? Did you miss me?"

"Maybe," she replied. "We've worked together for quite a while, and it's hard when patients suddenly decide that they're independent and don't need me anymore. It's almost like being jilted."

He burst out laughing, but, when he realized she was serious, he stopped. "I hadn't considered that, but you're right. You do spend a lot of time and effort invested in our care, and it really was thoughtless of me to not follow up."

She shrugged. "You and everybody else in this day and age," she muttered. "It's fairly common, even though I can't say I like it."

"Of course not," he admitted, "and it's a good reminder. I hadn't considered your feelings at all, and I'm sorry."

"You don't need to consider my feelings," she pointed out, "because I'm fine. I was just wondering if you were doing okay because you canceled, then never rescheduled. I don't have a recent follow-up on you, so I don't really know what shape you're in right now."

"I'm doing fine, as you can see."

"I can see, and I'm glad," she said, with a smile. "It still doesn't change the fact that you canceled the appointment."

He chuckled. "I did, but I promise I'll come back again." And he smiled at her. "It's really nice to see you out here, outside of the office, out where you're not forcing me to do shit that I don't want to do."

It was her turn to laugh. "You know it's for your own good."

"Of course I do, but since when is knowing that something is for your own good also easy to stomach?" He held out a hand to her.

She grabbed his hand, and the two of them walked together with a sense of peace and camaraderie. When they exited the forest, she stopped and gasped in awe at the lake before them.

He nodded. "Julie was right. This is spectacular."

CHAPTER 6

THE THREE OF them stayed at the lake for a couple hours, talking, laughing, and playing. They went for a swim in the freezing cold water, even Brutus. Of course Walton had to take off his prosthetic. They weren't in the water for long. When Chelsea came back out, having gone in wearing just her underwear, she was shivering. Even running around to dry off as much as possible, which Brutus thought was a fun game, she still shivered. When he looked at her with concern, she shrugged.

"I'll be fine, but I do think it's time to go back." She quickly pulled on the rest of her clothing, as they had no towels.

Walton looked over at her and laughed. "I never thought you would be one to jump in the lake like that."

"I wouldn't have thought I was either," she admitted, "but there is something about you."

"I think it's something about the atmosphere here," he noted, with a grin on his face. "It's very freeing. It's very open and caring."

"Except for those guys."

"Yes, except for those guys," he admitted. "But they won't be here forever, and it's really nice to see you in a more relaxed environment."

"Am I always uptight to you?" she asked curiously, as

they walked back at a rapid pace, compared to earlier, just because of the cold and being wet.

"No, I think you're just always hyper focused on the task at hand," he explained. "It's a very intense focus, which is what makes you so good at what you do."

She was still smiling and laughing when they walked back into the yard of the lodge.

The men were standing around discussing something in low voices, and silence fell when they saw them. As soon as Chad saw Brutus, he called him over in a harsh tone. Brutus walked over sedately, as if completely unfazed.

Chad spun on Walton. "What the fuck are you doing with my dog?"

"Your dog was out in the woods," Walton began. "You could at least say thank you that we brought him back with us." Chad looked down at the dog and raised his hand. Walton stepped forward and snapped in a waspish tone, "No, you don't."

Chad looked at him and glared. "You think you'll fucking stop me from disciplining my dog?"

"Until you show me papers that confirm he is your dog," Walton stated, pointing to Brutus, "I will guard that dog, the same way I did when I was in the military and trained these animals." His tone was hard and stern. "You will not abuse that animal."

"It's not your fucking animal."

"We can make a phone call right now and let the War Department sort it out. How's that?" As Walton spoke, Chad stumbled backward. Walton continued on. "What we'll do next is tear apart your life, as we look for anything incriminating as to how you got this dog, since his owner of record is in the hospital, after having the shit kicked out of him and his place robbed."

An ugly silence behind Chad was broken, as one of the men muttered, "Shit."

Chad turned and glared at his friend. "Just shut the fuck up," he roared. "And you," he said, turning back to Walton, "I had nothing to do with it."

"Yeah? Then where the hell did you get the dog?"

"You didn't have that dog a few days ago," noted Hawk. "We all saw you then as we flew in over a couple of days for this trip and you didn't have it."

Chad turned on him and asked, "What do you know? It's not as if you saw where I was staying this last month. You don't know shit about me."

"No, I don't, and for a hell of a lot of good reasons too," he muttered, as he walked toward the front doors of the lodge. "It was a fucking mistake coming up here."

"It was supposed to be a chance for us to let off some steam and to bond a little bit," Chad snarled, glaring at him as he continued to walk into the house. "Don't you ever fucking walk away from me."

At that, Hawk stiffened, then turned to face him. "Is that a warning? Or maybe I should ask if it's a threat? Because I really need to know just what the hell is going on here. At one point in time, we were all good friends."

"Yes, and then somebody killed Rudy," Darren stated, stepping forward, "and now we're at each other's throats."

"That's because the cops think one of us did it," Hawk snapped, "and I know I didn't, and I sure as hell don't want the cops looking at me for it."

"I didn't do it." Chad glared at Hawk. "You know me. Hell, you all know me."

"We also know that you've got one hell of a temper,"

George snapped at him. "If I find out you fucking beat up that old man to get his dog, I'll take you down myself," he vowed. "That old man was a war vet. I know that you really hate them, and it's all because you were turned down for entrance into the damn military, but you sure as hell shouldn't be going off and beating up people to get their goddamn dogs." And, with that, George turned his back on Chad deliberately and walked inside, right alongside Hawk.

Chelsea didn't know what to say; she was frozen in place. It was like watching a horrible play happen in front of her. Yet it was information they all needed, including the cops. If it ever came down to it, she and Rick and Julie and Walton would all likely be called in as witnesses to this nightmare. And Chelsea wasn't too thrilled about that either. As soon as she could, she raced inside and away from the chaos.

Julie met her in the kitchen. "Are you okay?" Julie asked in a low voice.

Chelsea nodded. "I am, but things are rough out there," she muttered. "Lots of accusations, nobody really fessing up to anything yet, although Chad doesn't have any ownership to the dog that he can prove."

At that, Julie glanced backward, with a worried expression on her face. "He's one of those dangerous guys with a short fuse and an unpredictable temper."

"I know," Chelsea agreed in a low tone.

"Would you mind putting on some tea?"

"I'm freezing. Let me go get into some dry clothes first."

At that, Julie looked at her. "What happened?"

She grinned. "I can't believe it myself, but we went for a swim."

"You what?"

The look of horror on her sister-in-law's face made Chelsea realize just how ludicrous it was to go swimming in freezing-cold water. "Honest to God, it was so much fun to just be out there," she shared, with a laugh. "I don't remember the last time I had a holiday where I could just forget about all kinds of crap. Even the dog enjoyed swimming with us. Then we come back here and found those guys fighting among themselves, and it's just horrifying."

Julie nodded. "Go on up and get changed. I'll get the teakettle going. We don't want you getting sick."

"No, I sure don't want to get sick," she agreed, with a laugh, "but I'm having a lot of fun, so I'm really glad I came."

At that, Julie smiled. "I'm really glad you came too." Then she stopped and winced. "But I wish you hadn't brought trouble with you."

She nodded. "I wish we hadn't either, but this was still a good thing for Brutus."

"Chad really doesn't have any rights to that dog?" Julie asked, peeking out the window.

"None that Walton can find, and Chad sure as hell isn't offering any proof. And any mention of the military or the cops coming to inspect what Chad was up to sends him into a tizzy."

"I wonder why," Julie noted in a wry tone.

Chelsea nodded. "He's not the kind of guy you want hanging around."

"No, he really isn't," Julie confirmed.

And, with that, Chelsea reminded Julie with a quick glance and a one-word question, "Tea?" Then she broke out laughing, as she raced up to her room.

WALTON STARED AT Chad straight-on, knowing perfectly well this man was not somebody you ever wanted to turn your back on. Walton was surprised and yet pleased when Rick came outside and stepped up beside him.

"Any problem here, gentlemen?" he asked in a calm, controlled tone.

Walton smirked. Rick used to be a counselor for children of all ages, but mostly for high school kids. It was pretty easy to see why somebody might want a change of career after doing that for many years. Yet it appeared Rick had picked up some valuable skills too. With two of the men inside, that left only two outside, Chad and Darren.

"No problem here," Darren noted, as he looked over at Chad. "Chad, you good?"

"Sure, I'm good, but this guy's trying to take my dog."

"If you think I have wronged you, let's talk ownership then," Walton suggested. "You give me names, dates, places, and documentation, all showing me that you are authorized to have this War Dog."

He glared at him. "It was a deal between friends," he muttered.

"What friend was that?"

At that point, Chad appeared stumped.

"Shit," Darren muttered. "If it isn't your dog, just give it back to him, man. You don't seem to give a shit about the dog anyway."

"What do you mean I don't give a shit about him?"

"You wanted him so you could play with him in the woods," Darren explained, "and it wasn't even sporting. You were always wondering what a War Dog could do against a bear or something. Jesus Christ, Chad, he's injured. You know he can't do anything to fight off a bear."

"It still would have been fun to see."

"No, it fucking wouldn't have been," Darren muttered. "You need your head examined."

"No, I fucking don't." He slammed his buddy with a fist to the gut.

Darren just blocked the hit and shook his head, then spoke to Walton. "Look. Chad hasn't had the animal for long, but I don't know that he's responsible for what happened to the owner."

"He better come up with a perfectly good reason why he's got the dog and how the owner ended up in the hospital," Walton stated. "That is definitely not something the government will let Chad walk away from, especially not when the Alaskan police are actively looking for the assailant of a war veteran."

At that, Darren winced. He shot his buddy a sideways glance. "I sure as hell hope it wasn't you, Chad, not when we've already got trouble."

"I didn't do anything," Chad said in a dark tone, "and it would be nice if somebody would ever fucking believe me."

"It depends on whether you deserve believing or not," Walton stated. "If you think about it, so far, we haven't heard anything but lies. I'm all for hearing the truth, but I'm not up for any more of your shit talk. Since you've been here, you've been nothing but a pain in the ass. I get that you think your shit doesn't stink and that the world should revolve around you, but it doesn't, and it won't. So, right about now, nobody wants to listen to any more of your crap."

Darren's eyes widened, and he hurriedly stepped away

from Chad, as if afraid an explosion was imminent.

Walton crossed his arms over his chest in a lazy move and just eyed Chad steadily. "So, speak up, or lose the damn dog right now."

"You can't fucking take the damn dog from me."

"Why? You don't have any proof that the dog is yours," Walton repeated, "so I really don't give a shit what you say."

Darren's jaw worked, and Chad curled his lips. "You don't have any fucking proof of all this bullshit that you're spouting either," Chad declared. "You just saw my damn dog and wanted it."

"It's not your dog." Walton pulled out his phone and quickly dialed.

"Whoa, whoa, whoa, who are you calling?" Chad asked nervously.

At his nervous tone Walton smiled at Chad. "You were looking for proof," Walton replied, with a casual glance, "about who I am and what I'm doing here. I will give you to my boss, Badger."

"*Badger*," he scoffed, "nobody fucking calls himself Badger."

"Yeah, do you know what a badger is?"

He frowned, "Yeah, I do. It's one of the fucking most dangerous animals in the world, and you never want to cross them. I'm not an idiot. I know what the fuck that is."

Walton gave him a slow smile. "Exactly." Badger answered his call, and Walton put it on Speakerphone. "Tell this dog-stealing asshole who I am and who I'm working with."

"The US War Department, asshole. Hand over the dog before things get worse for you. I hear you are under investigation for murder too. Did you also attack the War

Dog's owner and send him to the hospital? The Alaskan cops want to know."

Chad blinked several times, as comprehension dawned. "That's fucking bullshit," he said nervously, but he took a step back.

"No, it's not bullshit," Walton argued. "We take our animals seriously."

"You can have the thing then," he snarled at him. "Fucking thing doesn't listen anyway."

"He doesn't listen because you don't know what you're doing with him." Walton snapped his fingers and gave a downward hand signal. Brutus, a name Walton would have to change, raced over and dropped to the ground beside him.

Chad stared at Walton, his eyes widening.

Walton nodded. "These dogs are not to be trifled with. They're well trained, but they aren't something that you get to just have out here for sporting fun. What was that you said earlier? … Something about pitting him up against a grizzly bear or some such nonsense?"

Chad frowned at him, looked at the dog, and shrugged. "It's just fun, man. What the hell? It's just a dog."

"And that's why we know that you would never have been given this animal," Walton stated, with a wave of his hand. "*Never*, that's not what these War Dogs are bred for."

"So what? To hell with it and you. … I don't give a shit." Chad stomped up the front steps of the lodge. "This has turned out to be one fucking waste of a holiday."

"Did you get all that, Badger?"

"I sure did." And he ended the call, swearing a blue streak.

"You're the one who came up here to shoot things," snapped Chelsea from the doorway.

He glared at her. "Get the fuck out of my way, bitch." He nudged her aside, and, in an instant, Walton was right there between him and Chelsea.

"She's a lady, and you'll treat her like one," he uttered, his tone lethal and low. "If this is how you get along in life, I'm surprised you're not already behind bars, and that attitude will get you killed one day."

Chad stiffened and glared at him. "You don't know fuck about me. Now you've got your fucking dog, so get out of my fucking face." And, with that, he stormed inside and slammed the door.

Walton slowly turned and looked over at Rick. "You cool?"

Rick shrugged. "I wasn't expecting that to happen," he said, uncrossing his arms and approaching slowly. "You know he's dangerous."

"He's definitely dangerous," Walton stated agreeably, "as long as you know it too."

"Hell, as soon as I saw these guys and heard them, I understood they would be nothing but shit customers," Rick muttered. "But sometimes the shittiest of customers tip well, and I've got to tell you that business ain't what it used to be."

"Yet you told me everything was fine," Chelsea chided him. "I could have helped, you know."

"Helped with what?" he asked, looking over at her, his lips quirking. "I mean, you have the money you make, but it's not as if you have spare cash, and we've already accepted a lot of help from you."

"What about the marketing?" she muttered.

"We did get some bookings from that," he admitted, "and I'll talk to Julie more about it. The problem is, we didn't have the money to spend in order to market it properly."

"And if you don't spend the money, you don't get the guests, so you can turn around and market again."

He burst out laughing, wrapping an arm around her shoulders. "Let's go in and grab some coffee."

"Julie is making me a hot cup of tea," she said, looking over at Walton. "I went up and got changed," she muttered. "I was starting to get chilled pretty good."

At that, Rick looked down at her, then over at Walton. "Shit, you're wet."

"Yeah, I will get changed myself." Walton snapped his fingers, and Brutus raced to him, his tail wagging, happy as hell to have somebody talking to him in a language he understood.

Rick looked at him in amazement. "Is it really that easy?"

"No, it's not easy at all," Walton joked. "A hell of a lot of training goes into it."

Rick flushed. "I didn't mean it like that," he muttered, "but he looks to be a hell of a nice dog to have around.'

"He *is* a nice dog to have around," Walton agreed. "He's got excellent training and really good instincts. I'm really happy that I've got him out of that ugly scenario."

"I can't believe Chad let you just have him," Chelsea noted, frowning at him.

"Oh, I wouldn't say we're out of the woods yet," Walton cautioned. "I would say that Chad is pretty damn dangerous, and we'll have to watch every step we take to ensure Brutus here doesn't get an accidental bullet."

She stared at him, then glanced down at Brutus in horror. She crouched down, opening her arms as a signal to the dog. Brutus looked up at Walton for permission first, and he nodded. And Brutus raced toward her, looking for cuddles. "Oh my God," she said. "He's freaking beautiful."

"Isn't he," Walton agreed, "and incredibly well trained, even after those assholes tried to mess him up."

"Is he yours now?" she asked Walton.

"No, he's not." The saddest expression crept over her face, and he burst out laughing. "It completely depends on what's happening with his owner."

"Right, the poor man who got beaten up."

"Exactly. I don't know what the deal is there, and we do need to find out more about that, but, in the meantime," he added, "it will be a delight to have Brutus around." Walton gave a whistle, and Brutus raced over to him. "Almost everybody changes the name of the dog when they get them, usually something cuddlier than the original name," he explained, with a smile. "*Brutus* isn't a name we want him to have, but again it depends on his rightful owner."

"Right," she murmured, "let's hope he's got something a whole lot kinder." He looked over, then smiled. "At least a name that is a whole lot more realistic because he's not a brute, and also he's injured," she clarified, walking closer, studying his back leg. "We can probably do a lot to get that leg working a little bit better." She squatted beside the dog, checking his back leg.

CHAPTER 7

CHELSEA'S MIND RACED with all the possible ways to get some of that mobility back for Brutus. When she heard a chuckle, she looked up to see Walton staring at her, a big affectionate smile on his face. "What?" she asked, frowning at him.

"*You*. You're already figuring out how to fix him."

She flushed. "I'm not trying to fix him. I'm trying to improve his mobility."

"Right," he said, with a nod. "Seems to be the same thing to me. What about you? How does it appear to you?" he asked Rick.

"Looks like the same damn thing to me." Rick nodded. "Sure as hell does."

She groaned. "It's not the same damn thing," she muttered, "and, besides, it's a good thing."

"Oh, it's absolutely a good thing, no doubt," Walton agreed. "You figure out what exercises he needs, and I'll figure out a way for him to get it done in training."

"Perfect," she said, now looking at Brutus with a big smile. "Sounds as if you've got the best of both worlds there, sweetie." And she patted him on the head, then hugged him close. She turned, looked back at Rick, and asked, "Now, how about some coffee or tea?"

"Hey, I've been standing here waiting for you to get your

shit together," he muttered. As she walked closer, he added in a low tone, "Seems as if you're getting pretty involved."

"Always was pretty involved," she admitted. "You just don't realize how much." He frowned, then glanced over at Walton. She shrugged and added, "I've been working with Walton for quite a few months now, until he decided not to come back."

Walton snorted. "It's not that I decided to *not* come back," he argued, "but I had to get a few more surgeries done. Doctor's orders. And Kat needed it done before trying out some improved prosthetics."

Her gaze widened. "Why didn't you tell me about the *plural* surgeries?"

He gave her a smile. "Not anything major."

"We'll have to talk about that," she said, shooting him a look. "I know I graduated you out of all the major work we were doing, but you were still supposed to come back for tune-ups."

"I promise that I'll be back for tune-ups."

She snorted. "I think I've heard that a time or two." They all stepped inside the lodge.

"I'll go get changed and meet you back here for that coffee." With that, Walton climbed the stairs to his room.

"At one point in time they do graduate out of your care though, don't they?" Rick asked, as he and his sister wandered toward the kitchen.

"Sure." Chelsea scrunched up her nose, lowering her voice. "At some point in time they've done physio, but it takes an amazing amount of time to get to that level of discharge, and Walton has worked incredibly hard, so he did make it," she explained. "Yet he was supposed to still come back for periodic checks."

"You think he had those additional surgeries?" Rick asked, stopping in the hallway to face Chelsea.

"I assume so. He just told us that he did."

"You trust him?" Rick asked. "Stan knows him, but being in the service, his injury… could have changed him."

She sensed something deeper in his question. She looked at him carefully and then nodded. "Yes," she replied in a low voice, "I trust him completely."

"Good," Rick stated, "because he's taken on some ugly turf here."

"I know," she murmured, "but these guys weren't very nice to me … or to Julie."

At that, Rick frowned. "Have they been mean to her? Did they say something to her?" he asked, the outrage building in his tone.

Chelsea snorted. "You knew they were hassling me, so why didn't you think they would do the same to Julie?" When he spun and glared at her, she sighed, lifted her hand in peace and added, "I get it. I get it. As far as I know, Julie's okay, but these guys aren't exactly the kind of men I would want around her or me."

"I know," Rick grumbled, "and it is one of the things we've been talking about. *Seriously.*"

"But you love this business."

"I do," he agreed, hanging his head, "but it's very erratic, not something we can count on all year long." He hesitated and then added, "We have to look to the future."

"Don't we all," Chelsea muttered. She looked around to see Julie coming toward them. "There she is," Chelsea noted, with a smile. Catching the look on her brother's face as he glanced over at his wife, Chelsea's heart squeezed with hope. If only somebody looked at her that way. The thought came and went in a second, and it left her longing.

Julie smiled up at him. Rick pulled her close and then turned to Chelsea. "Besides, we haven't had a chance to tell you something."

"Oh, yeah?" Chelsea teased, as they all moved closer. "What's that?"

"Not now," Julie said hurriedly. Rick frowned at her, and Julie shrugged. "I'm sure there's a better time for telling them." Rick wanted to argue with her, but she shook her head with a firm shrug.

Curious, Chelsea looked from one to the other, not sure what was going on. Then Walton rejoined them, bringing up the rear with Brutus. "Anything that you guys want to tell me, I'm okay to hear it," Chelsea suggested.

"Later," Julie repeated. "It's fine, so let's just talk later." And, with that, she brushed it off and added, "Come on. Let's get you some hot tea."

As if realizing something had changed Julie's attitude, Rick quickly slipped ahead of her and walked into the kitchen.

Following behind him, Chelsea noted that the group of men were all standing around in the kitchen, not arguing, but not comfortable either. As soon as Walton walked in with Brutus at his side, one of the other men questioned him.

"What the hell are you doing stealing that dog off Chad? I'm not sure I believe he did it, regardless it's not of your damn business," Darren was mad as hell. "I've got a mind to punch the shit out of you for that."

"Go ahead," Walton replied in a lazy tone of voice. "I've got no problem punching you back."

Darren stared at him. "I'm totally okay for a dust-up,"

he said, a growl forming in the back of his throat. "And I know perfectly well that my buddies are too."

Walton laughed. "So you threaten me with a dustup, but want these other guys to back you up because of what? You can't handle me on your own?" Walton asked in a taunting tone.

Darren glared at him. "No, but they're my friends."

"Yeah, friends who may have killed one of your other friends?" Walton asked incredulously. "Is that what it takes to be a friend of yours? Is it some rite of passage for you? Go beat up an old man, steal his dog, then go kill a friend of yours who doesn't follow along with your little game or some bullshit like that? What the hell is wrong with you guys?"

The men stiffened at Walton's words, and utter silence fell, as they all ingested what Walton just said.

Darren added, "And what the fuck do you know about our friend?"

"It's not as if we don't hear you guys all spouting out that shit when you're sitting here," Walton pointed out, glaring at Darren. "You've been talking about it nonstop, how you didn't kill Rudy, but one of these other guys did."

"You think I'm thrilled about that?" Darren asked.

"The way you guys treat the dog, the way you talk about killing animals, the way you treat women? Hell, for all I know, you'll all end up killing somebody in some initiation practice, you sick motherfuckers."

The men just stared at Walton in shock.

Chad straightened up slowly. "Look. I don't want any of you talking to this asshole," he said to his friends. "He'll get his."

At that, Walton turned that lazy gaze on him. "Another threat?" he asked, as he pulled out his phone.

"What now? Will you call your Badger friend again?"

"Nope, I'll go directly to the cops, since they're keeping an eye on you guys already. They might want to know your current whereabouts." When Walton got a voicemail prompt, all he said was, "Call me. Got info for you on the location of four suspects." Then he pocketed his phone.

"What the hell do you know about it?" Chad snapped.

"When I realized you'd stolen the dog, I did a background check on you," Walton explained, without taking his gaze off Chad, "and believe me that I learned more than I wanted to."

Chad straightened slowly. "Then you also know I'm not one to fuck around."

"Yeah, I can see that. That's how you got the dog, right? You beat up some old guy, a retired military veteran, in order to get an animal you wanted. Then you tell your friends you didn't kill your other *friend*," he explained, with air quotes. "But why the hell would anybody believe you? Your whole life is one big criminal record, starting with your juvie records."

"My juvie records are sealed."

"They were unsealed when you were charged with that last burglary."

"I've not been convicted of that."

"No, but it's pending. The cops just haven't followed through yet."

"They don't have enough evidence," he snapped.

Chelsea saw the fury burning up inside Chad. Chelsea walked up and slipped her hand into Walton's. "Do you want a coffee, honey?" she asked.

He glanced down at her, smiled, then squeezed her fingers. "Thank you, that would be nice."

She headed to the sideboard and poured him a cup, bringing it back to him.

"And how about dinner?" he asked, breathing on the hot brew. "Any idea when that is?"

"Coming up soon," she replied, looking at him curiously. "Why?"

"Just hungry," he said, with a smile.

"God, you guys make me sick," Chad stated. "You're acting as if you're something special, and really all you are is a nosy jerk who thinks he can piss off everybody."

"I don't care about pissing off everybody, but, seeing as you've got your pants on fire, I did a pretty good job with you, wouldn't you say?"

"You're just asking for it, aren't you?" Chad glared at him.

"I am prepared to defend myself and the people I love. Go do the math if you want," Walton added. "I've fought plenty of men in my time." He sipped his coffee, staring down Chad. "I know exactly what's involved, and, if we want to take it down, we take it down. However, if you think I'll stop pursuing justice when I know you're the kind of scum who would beat up an old veteran to steal his dog, you're wrong. And having mentioned that, it's not that big of a leap to consider that you killed that friend of yours, Rudy. So, I'm not letting you off the hook on that one either. If the cops think you did it and want you back in for an interview, I'll ensure you end up back in."

"No fucking way, they told me that I was free and clear."

"No, they didn't." Walton snorted. "You can let all your buddies think that's true, but what you were told was that you could go on a hunting trip, not that you were off the hook for any investigations. Or off the hook for owning a firearm. So I presume your weapons 'belong' to someone else? The cops just weren't doing anything about you yet, while they're still gathering evidence," Walton shared, with a hard tone. He glanced over at the others, who were all staring at their buddy. "*All* of you are still under investigation for Rudy's murder, and not a one of you is in the clear yet."

"We should be," Darren declared, staring at him. "I didn't have anything to do with Rudy's death or beating up some guy to get a dog."

"Glad to hear that," Walton replied, "because the cops don't really believe you."

"Why not?" Darren asked. "They already came and talked to me, but they didn't arrest me or anything. I didn't do anything, so I wasn't worried about it. So what the hell do you mean?"

"It means that they're still looking into it, and they'll know soon enough that you're all up here right now," he shared, as he hugged the coffee cup, warming his hands.

Chelsea watched him and the casual manner he used to handle these men, while inside, she was just waiting for it all to blow up, unsure which way it would go. These four men had guns all around the place, and Rick did too, but that was a different story. She just wasn't sure what the hell would happen, and she couldn't quite relax as all this testosterone was barreling around the room in a very uncomfortable way. Yet Walton seemed to have no problem with it at all.

The men looked at each other, and finally Hawk muttered, "This is just fucked up. I didn't have anything to do with it. Chad wanted to talk to us about it and seems to think that one of us had something to do with Rudy's death."

"Did you?" Walton asked.

"No, I just told you that I didn't. I didn't have anything to do with it, and I wouldn't. Rudy was a friend of mine, a good friend," he muttered. "It broke my damn heart to hear what happened to him. If I found out any one of you assholes hurt him … Jesus Christ. What's the point of having friends if you hurt them?" he asked, staring at each of his buddies.

"I didn't hurt him," Darren replied defensively.

"Maybe not," Hawk muttered, "but it sure seems somebody knows more than they're saying. Hell, even this guy knows more." He pointed to Walton. Hawk then turned to face Chad. "Did you beat up that old man for his dog?"

"No, I didn't fucking beat him up for his dog." But the way he spoke made the others turn and stare at him.

"So, you did beat him up, but not for his dog?" Hawk asked. "The dog was just there, so you took it?"

Chad flushed at that. "I ain't saying nothing," he snapped, glaring at them. "I didn't fucking steal the dog."

"Meaning that the old guy wasn't capable of looking after the dog anymore, so you just figured the dog should be yours?" asked Hawk, staring at him. "Jesus Christ, Chad. It's no wonder we're always in so much trouble just because of you. That was a shit move."

"Hey, … the old man pissed me off. He was a fucking nobody, and he was trying to rip me off. You know I won't let that happen."

"Rip you off how?"

"He was supposed to sell me some of that wood he had in the backyard. Remember all that cherry?"

"What happened then?"

"I was looking for some wood for some projects, and he

had all that cherrywood. I told him that I wanted it, but he wouldn't sell it to me."

"Yeah, you probably didn't offer him anything."

"I didn't want a whole lot, but I was willing to give him a fair price, but he wouldn't sell it to me. So what? We might have gotten into a bit of an argument, and he fell backward, but that ain't my fault."

The others groaned. "Jesus Christ, why would you get into that kind of trouble right now? You know the cops are already looking at us."

"They're not looking at me," Chad declared, with a sneer. "I told you that I didn't have anything to do with it."

"That's what we *all* said," Hawk reminded him. "Every fucking one of us said the same thing, but you think the cops will believe any of us when you're spouting all these lies?"

"I'm not lying though," Chad declared, staring at Hawk. "I didn't kill Rudy, so I'm not worried about it," he snapped.

"Now they know that you beat up this old man."

"I didn't fucking beat him up, okay? And, besides, it's not as if he would need the dog. He was just lying there."

"And yet"—Walton studied him—"the guy wasn't just lying there. He was really banged up."

"Yeah, so what? I fucking told you that he fell," Chad snapped, "so it's not as if that's my problem."

"Meaning that he fell, and you didn't do anything to make him fall or to split apart his face?"

"No, I didn't," Chad snapped, glaring at him. "It's not my fault the old man tripped."

"The old man *tripped?*" Walton repeated, giving Chad a look. "The old man was in a wheelchair. Are you telling us that a man in wheelchair *tripped and fell?*"

Again came dead silence. When all his friends turned

and looked at him, Chad raised both hands. "But he didn't have to be in that wheelchair. He got up to show me something, and he was livid, pissed, and tried to throw a punch. I pushed him back into his wheelchair, and the wheelchair toppled to the side, and he fell, okay? So it had nothing to do with me."

The other men just stared at Chad in shock. "Jesus Christ," Hawk muttered, running his fingers through his hair. "What the hell, man? You didn't even … didn't you try and get him back on his feet or help him?"

"No, he was fucking furious and trying to hit me."

"So, of course, you called for help for him then, right?" Chelsea asked, staring at him in shock.

He glared at her. "It's none of your fucking business what I did."

She gulped and then nodded. "Which means you didn't. You just left the old man, who was already in great physical distress, on the ground. You just left him there." She hesitated, groaned, then shook her head. "Oh, God. Did you feel as if you needed to give him that one final kick to his face in a temper fit as you walked out?" He turned and looked at her in horror, and she nodded slowly. "I was afraid of that," she muttered. "So, not only did you *not* get him any help when he was already down and helpless, but you kicked the shit out of his face too."

"I did not, okay? I lost my temper, and I kicked him once. That was it."

"Just once?" she asked, glaring at him. "What kind of lowlife are you?" She couldn't stand around and stomach this asshole any longer. She spun on her heel and left the kitchen, where she didn't have to see him.

She was sick and tired of listening to him. As she walked

into the living room, she found Julie staring out the window, her hand on her belly. Chelsea stopped, stared at her. With an insight of knowing, she whispered, "You're pregnant, aren't you?"

WALTON KEPT HIS eye on the group of men throughout dinner and the rest of the evening. They all seemed to be stiff, not even talking to each other, but, more than that, eyeing him warily. He'd become the enemy to all of them. He understood that and was happy to play the role, but he also knew he didn't dare turn his back on any of them.

If the Mississippi detective Walton had talked to was correct, one of them was a killer, and the others might not even know. Walton got up to help clear the table, but Julie waved him back.

"It's fine. I've got this."

He looked over at her and replied, "You know it doesn't hurt to let someone pitch in." He carried the dishes into the other room. Ahead of him, he saw Chelsea talking to her brother, as they merrily loaded up the dishwasher. He quickly jumped in to lend a hand.

She smiled at him. "Thank you."

"Don't sound so surprised," Walton replied. "I am housebroken." She burst into peals of laughter, as he grinned at her. "You should do that more often."

"What?" she asked, stopping suddenly, looking at him in confusion.

He rolled his eyes, fully aware that her brother was listening to their interactions. "Laugh—uncontrollably carefree and unrestrained."

Her gaze turned inward, and she nodded. "I don't do it all that often, do I?" she asked pensively. "You grow up, get disconnected, and forget about it."

"Nothing to get disconnected about," he said, looking at her. "You're young, beautiful, talented, gifted. You really do have a lot of reasons to love life."

"I do love life," she agreed, flushing slightly, "and thank you for the compliment."

"Wasn't a compliment," he said cheerfully. "It was the truth." And, with that, he swung around and announced, "If you guys don't mind, I'll take Brutus outside for an evening walk and then hit the sack." When Chelsea eyed him, he shrugged. "The leg has had better days."

"Right. I'll check on you before I go to bed."

He snorted. "Why is that?"

"Because if it seizes up, you won't get out of bed tomorrow."

"I won't argue that point," he muttered. With a smile at Rick and Julie, Walton headed to the back door, opened it, and called for Brutus. Walton really hated that name, but it wasn't the time to confuse the dog with another one. He was just avoiding most of it by using as many hand signals as he could.

Outside was a seriously beautiful evening. He stopped and took several deep breaths, absolutely loving the fresh scents. When he heard someone call out to him, he turned to see Rick walking toward him. "So where are the women?" Walton asked.

"I've got them together. And Julie knows where I keep the guns, and she's a good shot."

"Good to hear. ... You're really blessed to have this place."

Rick sighed and nodded. "I've felt that way a few times myself."

"So, you should," Walton agreed. "Sometimes it's worth everything, and then sometimes you have to assess what it's really worth."

Rick laughed. "God, … now you sound like my sister."

"She's good people," Walton replied.

"Yeah, I was wondering about that."

Walton looked over at him. "Wondering about what? Whether she's good people?" he asked him in amusement.

Rick rolled his eyes. "No, I hate to be an overbearing big brother, but …"

"But *What are my intentions?*"

"Yeah, something like that." Rick shuffled uneasily on his feet. "I know that she'll want to shoot me for this."

"Yeah, she probably would," Walton confirmed, "but I understand that you're worried about her."

"It's not even so much that I'm worried about her. It's just that this happened kind of fast, didn't it?"

"I'm not so sure about that," Walton countered, yet with a smile on his face. "We went to high school together. Then after I got back from the military, we had a hell of a rapport when she was my therapist. I just didn't figure it was fair to combine business with pleasure."

"That's interesting. I'm not sure too many guys would have cared." Rick studied Walton closely.

"Maybe not, but I was more concerned about making sure I didn't end up as some … pity piece."

"Ah." Rick nodded. "That wouldn't appeal to me either."

"Exactly." Walton smiled. "Still, Chelsea will be pissed hearing that."

Rick burst out laughing. "Yeah, no doubt. She's something though. She's good people."

"I mentioned that already," Walton noted, with a nod, "and we're just exploring things."

"It seems to be more than that. Exploring things is … I don't want to say *serious*, but definitely denotes a strong interest."

"Sure, *strong interest* is a good phrase for it," Walton agreed, still smiling. "She's helping me out by bringing me up here. I'm feeling a bit on the shitty side because I know I'm screwing up all your plans."

"No, you're not screwing up the plans," Rick replied. "I was hoping these guys would be a little easier to work with, but sometimes you get a group in and just nothing you can do about them."

"And that's true," Walton murmured, "but they're not all shit, and I'm not sure all of these guys are shit. It's more a case of figuring out which ones are any good and which ones aren't."

"I never did have much of a bullshit meter," Rick said, with a smile. "I would like to think I know decent from not, but it's often very hard to read people, especially when they come up here looking to have fun and to let off a little steam."

"Yeah, looking to have fun and letting off a little steam is one thing, but having killers in your backyard? … That's a whole different deal."

"Are you serious about that?" Rick asked.

Walton nodded. "I am unfortunately, and I would even say *dead serious*, but that sounds overly dramatic. Yet another guy in their group, Rudy, was murdered, and all of them are under suspicion. It's likely that one of them is the killer."

"Shit," Rick muttered, "and, even if one of them did do it, no way to know which one?"

"Up here, you really don't want to get into those kinds of accusations," Walton pointed out, "since these guys tend to be a little quick to launch off the mark and a little bit trigger-happy. It's also one of the reasons I wanted to ensure Chad didn't have a War Dog at his disposal to go kill somebody with."

At that, Rick stopped and looked at him. "Do you think that dog would kill?"

Walton faced him. "All dogs would kill under the right circumstances, doesn't need to be a War Dog." Then he sighed. He wasn't sure if he should be so candid, but it was his place. "However, War Dogs are specifically taught self-defense and to be aggressive as needed from a very young age," he murmured. "That doesn't mean they're killers though."

Rick pondered that and nodded. "I guess that makes sense, though you had me scared there for a few minutes. I am nervous to have them around family."

"Me too, and Brutus is also injured," he pointed out.

"Right, and that should matter."

"It does matter. It matters a lot because he was injured because of us," Walton shared, "and that's something that people don't recognize either."

"What do you mean, *because of us*?" Rick asked in confusion.

"He was bred to go to war, and these War Dogs are the ones that generally end up saving us," Walton explained, "and often they get caught in the backfire. As much as we might want to save them, we can't save them all. Sometimes we can't save any of them. Very few of the K9s make it back home."

"Right. I don't even want to think about that," Rick noted.

Walton nodded. "We put all that time and effort into training an animal, and we're not technically allowed to get attached to them, which is a sad state of affairs. We're supposed to see them as weapons or tools," he added, with a flat look toward the dog, "and it's damn hard."

"I can imagine. I'm not sure I get it like you do, but I do understand."

"We spend time training to get an animal to do exactly what we need it to do, and then we're supposed to send it out into a war, where it's either likely to get killed or to be where something else could happen to it." Walton shook his head. "It's not for the faint of heart, and I did it for a long time, knowing that I was giving the dogs their best chance of survival, but that doesn't mean it was easy."

"No, hell no," Rick agreed, with a headshake. "I don't think I could do it."

"I did it for a while, and then I just couldn't do it anymore," Walton shared. "And that's just part of what goes wrong in our world so often." He stared off into the distance. "I can't explain it to somebody who hasn't been there because it's just hard to get anybody to understand how devastating that whole military life can be."

"But you're home now," Rick noted, "and you're recuperating."

"Yeah, more or less." Walton laughed. "Though your sister wants to see me back in for more physical therapy."

"Yeah, she would," Rick agreed, with a knowing smile, "but I'm pretty sure it's because she wants to see you, more of you."

"I hope so," Walton replied. They walked around the property in the moonlight. When he was ready to head back to the house, he called Brutus over with a whistle. Brutus looped toward them, his tail wagging.

"He's sure taken to you," Rick said. "Was he one of the dogs that you worked with over there?"

"No, I don't think so. You would think that maybe it would be easy to recognize him, but I worked with over one thousand K9s, so I can't be sure. Some were in my care for a little bit. Sometimes I assigned them to other trainers. Sometimes I was off on missions myself, while other trainers worked with the K9s," he added, with a smile, "but I certainly recognize his type."

"It's a good thing you did. He'll have a hell of a lot better life with you."

"That depends. I can't request to keep the dog until I know what the deal is with his owner. He was adopted by someone, and, until that is sorted out, I have only temporary custody of Brutus."

"Was the guy really beaten up?"

Walton nodded. "Yeah, and way more than just falling out of his wheelchair," he noted in disgust.

"Shit," Rick muttered, "that doesn't make me feel any better. Not exactly the kind of guys we want to have around here with the women."

"No, and that's another reason I brought it up. You need to keep an eye on Julie."

He spun and glared at him. "What do you mean by that?"

He hesitated, thinking about the wisdom of saying what he wanted to say. "I know she's pregnant, and I know that she's struggling emotionally with some of it. I'm not saying that's the reason for it. All I'm saying is that the men are a little on the rough side, and I don't want them thinking they can get away with manhandling anyone around the lodge."

"I'll kill them myself," Rick declared.

Walton nodded. "I understand the sentiment, but I don't want you going there either. I'm just saying this as a word of warning. Just keep an eye on her."

"I always do, and we have a certain security mind-set, but now you are scaring the crap out of me."

"I'm not trying to do that, but I felt I should give you a heads-up."

"It feels like more than that."

"Fine, so take it any way you want, but do keep an eye on them around the lodge."

"You're telling me that Julie's in danger?"

"No, I'm not telling you that specifically," he replied, turning to look at him. "I'm just saying that I don't like the way these men treat animals, and, after having a chance to do some eavesdropping on them today, I suspect that at least some of them, maybe more than some of them, don't treat women very well either."

"Shit." They walked back toward the house, and Rick glared at him as they walked closer to the back steps. "How the hell am I supposed to sleep now?"

Walton burst out laughing. "I'm not saying any imminent attack or anything is coming. I'm just saying, let's not put Julie into any situation that could cause her to lose the baby."

"That would be really bad," he noted glumly.

"She has had a hard time in that department?"

"We've been trying for a long time, and this is the first pregnancy that's made it this far. I wanted to tell Chelsea about it tonight, but Julie didn't want me to, … just in case."

Walton nodded. "I presume Chelsea knows?"

"I have no idea." He turned and looked at Walton in confusion. "But if you know, … I thought Julie or Chelsea must have told you."

He shook his head. "No, I'm just one of those guys who senses that sort of thing."

"You can tell when somebody's pregnant?" Rick asked, his eyes widening.

"Yeah, it's something we used to do with the War Dogs all the time. I don't want to say I had a perfect score, but I was about 99 percent right when it came to that."

"Or is that just because they were no longer in heat," Rick suggested, with a note of humor.

"It could be." Walton smiled at Rick. "It was a bit of a joke among us. Yet I can see Julie and recognize it. Another word of advice, don't say that to her."

"No, I wouldn't do that," Rick muttered. "I'm not that stupid."

The two of them were chuckling as they walked in the back door to find both Julie and Chelsea waiting for them.

"Now, wouldn't it be nice if we knew exactly why you guys were laughing," Chelsea said, looking at them suspiciously.

Walton frowned at her. "Good Lord, why would you want to know that?" She frowned back at him, and he nodded. "See? Absolutely nothing to worry about."

"*Huh*," Julie muttered, "I don't agree with *nothing to worry about*, but you're definitely on the scary side."

"Not me." Walton smiled at her and called out good night to the others. Then, with Chelsea beside him and

Brutus bringing up the rear, they climbed the stairs to their rooms.

As they got into their rooms, Chelsea began, "I had a talk with my sister-in-law."

"Yeah, did she tell you that she's pregnant?" Chelsea raised both hands, frowning. He shrugged. "It's pretty obvious."

"Holy crap, don't say that to any pregnant woman before she's even told anybody," she muttered.

"No, I won't." Walton held up his hand. "But she is, isn't she?"

"Yes, and she's both terrified and worried."

"Of course. I was talking to Rick about it."

"Wow, that's very unusual for him too."

"I did say that he needed to keep an eye on her, and not necessarily because she was pregnant. It's been on my mind since I noticed her."

Chelsea snorted. "I'm sure that went over like a ton of bricks."

"Yeah, maybe not the best thing to have mentioned," he noted, with a smile in her direction, "but I had good intentions."

"*Sure.*" She gave him an eye roll. "Everybody says shit like that, but ..."

"Hey, said with the best of intentions," he protested. "I'm not here to cause any trouble. Well, any more trouble."

"Glad to hear it," she muttered, waving her hands. She was irritated, and he could see it. "Yet it does seem as if you're dishing out all kinds of trouble."

"No, I'm not," he argued, with a headshake. "Honestly, I'm not. I'm just trying to solve some problems."

"How's that working for you?" she asked, with a laugh.

"Oh, it's been easier at other times in my life," he conceded, with a smile, "but still, we'll be doing just fine," he shared, glancing at her. "How about you?"

"I'm wary, nervous, upset, and absolutely ecstatic about Brutus here," she replied. At her mention of his name, Brutus came over for cuddles. "He's one hell of a dog," she murmured.

"He is," Walton agreed. "He's got an injury holding him back a bit, and I know how that feels, but he's still valiant." Walton grinned at her. "And Brutus's heart's in the right place too."

"Absolutely." She looked down at Walton's leg and added, "You need to get that prosthetic off."

"I do, and that'll take a little more energy than I have, but I'll get there."

"No, sit down," she ordered, and she gave him a light push. He let himself topple backward onto the bed, and, with her help, he got the prosthetic off. She frowned as she stared at the stump. "That doesn't look very happy."

"No, maybe not," he noted, as he studied it himself, "but it doesn't look that bad."

"*That bad?*" she repeated, with a snort. "As if you can measure it that way."

"Right, but you know sometimes it does seem like it."

"*Not that bad* isn't quite good enough for me," she stated, chewing on her words. "I do have some cream with me. I'll be back in a sec." She quickly disappeared into her side of the room, grabbed the cream, and came back, smiling up at him. "I did remember to bring it."

"Why would you bring that on a trip?"

"Instincts. You never know when you'll get a sprain or an injury," she explained, again rolling her eyes. "This is both cooling and healing." She quickly worked it into his stump, and he closed his eyes at the relief. "See? It feels better, doesn't it?"

He nodded. "It absolutely does."

"Good. Now get some sleep, and, if you need something, you'll give me a shout, right?"

"I don't need anything," he replied in bemusement, as he looked at her.

"But even if you did," she asked, with a sigh, "you wouldn't call out, would you?"

"I don't know. I've never been in that position."

She studied him for a long moment. "You're not alone anymore, you know?" And, on that note, she turned and walked into her room.

CHAPTER 8

CHELSEA WOKE THE next morning, yawned, and stretched, and then the memories from the night before came flooding back. It was sad to hear Walton talk as if he had nobody. Yet, she supposed, in Walton's mind, that's exactly what he did have—nobody. No matter what she felt about him, what he was thinking was muddy as hell.

She got out of bed and knocked on the connecting door to his room, but she got no answer. Frowning, she popped open the internal door and peered in, but his room was empty. "Damn it," she muttered. She dressed and raced downstairs to find Rick and Julie sitting at the kitchen table, having a serious talk. "Oops, am I interrupting?"

They looked up at her and shook their heads. "Of course not," Julie said warmly, then hopped up and walked over to the coffee pot. "Of course you're not interrupting. Come on in."

Chelsea hesitated because it was obviously a fairly serious discussion. "I was wondering where Walton has gone."

"He took Brutus outside," Rick replied, twisting in his chair to look at her. "He wanted us to let you sleep."

"Of course he did," she muttered, with a grin. "That man …"

"That man is looking after you," Julie stated in a jokingly cross tone of voice.

"Of course he is," Chelsea grumbled, with an eye roll. "He feels bad about ruining what's going on here."

"He shouldn't feel bad about it," Rick shared, with a casual wave of his hand. "It's not his fault."

"No, but I think he feels as if it's his fault because of the mess that is happening now."

"It's got nothing to do with his coming here, and it's a mess that needed to happen anyway," Julie stated, with a shrug. "It's not his fault at all, and we don't want him feeling that way."

"That's good. I'll tell him that, if and when I ever get a chance to see him again," she grumbled, with a sigh.

"Yeah, that's the trouble. When you find a good man, you've got to keep him," Julie teased, now laughing. "They tend to disappear all too quickly."

"You think he's a good one?" Chelsea asked.

"Oh, I know he is," Julie declared. "Anybody who cares for animals like he does is hard to go wrong with."

"Yeah, that's what I thought," Chelsea admitted, shooting her sister-in-law a bright grin, as Chelsea headed to the back door, her cup of coffee in hand. "Maybe I'll see if he's outside somewhere, and you guys can go back to whatever deep-seated problem you're dealing with."

"Maybe it's a problem that's your problem," Rick noted, holding Julie's hand.

Chelsea knew that protective gesture he made whenever he was feeling defensive. She stopped and studied him carefully. "What does that mean?"

He shrugged. "Apparently you heard it from Julie."

He was mentioning their pregnancy. "I did," she confirmed, her face beaming. She grinned at her sister-in-law. "Is it okay if I say something now?" Julie laughed and nodded. Chelsea raced over and gave her brother a great big hug. "I'm so thrilled for you guys."

He laughed and hugged her back. "I knew that you knew," he replied, "but did you know that Walton knew?"

"Yeah, he told me last night. Apparently he figured it out the day we arrived. He's kind of scary that way," she noted, with a smile. "*Very accurate intuition*, or at least that's how he put it."

"If he guessed, … that's pretty crazy," Julie noted. "I'm not showing." Then she frowned and glared at Rick. "Or am I?"

"No, you're not," he confirmed, patting her hand.

Julie snorted, turned to Chelsea and asked forcefully, "Am I?"

"Nope, not yet," she declared, "and no need to make a fuss. It is too bad though. Can't wait until I can see you all pudgy with baby."

Julie grinned. "Me either," she added excitedly.

"What? And here I thought if I had told you that you were pudgy or round with baby, you would have torn me to shreds." Rick frowned. "But she says it, and it's totally fine?"

"Of course it's totally fine," Julie replied. "And it would have been totally fine with you too, if you told the truth, but you didn't." She gave him a severe look. "So, yeah, you're still in the doghouse."

He raised both hands, shaking his head. "I guess that's my life for the next few months, with hormones and all."

"Yeah, it sure is," Chelsea teased, chuckling as she stepped onto the outside deck. There was a crispness to the air, almost a chill that was stunningly beautiful, yet empty. She glanced around, walking along the perimeter of the veranda that wrapped around the entire front of the house, looking for Walton, but she saw no sign of him.

Frowning, she headed back around to the front of the house to see Rick step out. "No sign of him," she muttered, with a sinking feeling.

"Oh, he wanted to take the dog out for a nice walk, so I don't know how long that'll be."

"What about Chad and his friends?" she asked.

"They all took off hunting this morning," Rick shared, "and believe me that we're not at all unhappy about that."

She nodded. "Good enough, I think," she muttered, "but …" Then she frowned. "Why is it that doesn't feel very good?"

"I have no idea what to say to that. The sooner they're out of my hair," Rick muttered, "the sooner life can get back to normal."

"Right," she muttered.

As she turned to look once again for Walton, she saw something in the trees move. Frowning, she stared and thought she saw someone tall and slender. She pointed it out to Rick, but he wasn't looking in that direction. By the time she turned back to whoever it was, they were gone again.

"What am I looking at?" Rick asked.

"Maybe George? I don't know," she said suddenly, "but I swear to God somebody was in the bushes over there."

"Where?"

She pointed off to the left, where a copse of trees stood.

He frowned. "All I see are trees. If somebody was there, it could have been Walton."

"No. Walton is heavier than whoever I caught a glimpse of," she muttered. In the distance she heard a gunshot and then a second one. She froze and turned to look at Rick. "Are they hunting this close to the lodge?"

His face grim, he shook his head. "They shouldn't be." He swore under his breath. "They sure as hell, sure as shit shouldn't be. You stay here with Julie."

And, with that, Rick nudged her inside, grabbed his own hunting rifle and headed out into the early morning air.

WALTON KEPT HIS distance from the hunting party that had taken off earlier this morning. He knew in which direction they had gone, and they were loudly traipsing around, making enough noise that the wild animals would be completely safe from them. It wasn't that a ton of skill was required for hunting, but a few basics on being quiet to let the animals come out and eat their morning breakfast or hit the local watering hole were useful. It was generally a good rule to go by, but these guys? As soon as they got out here, they broke down into yelling and arguing.

If they were friends, as in real friends, Walton would be surprised. They were bonded by a tragedy or a crime between them that none of them knew how to get out of. Walton was afraid that the only way anybody would get out of it was the wrong way.

Keeping Brutus close to his side, Walton walked outside, enjoying the early morning weather, giving the dog a chance to exercise and to loosen up his leg for the day, same as for Walton. It was always harder when you had a missing or damaged limb because the other limb had to do extra work to compensate. So, to get them both loosened up for the day required a little bit of intentional work.

Most people didn't have to think about that. They got out of bed knowing that, within a few minutes, their body would be turned on and ready to go. However, in Walton's case, turning it on wasn't quite the same thing.

He called Brutus to him, and they slowly headed back toward the lodge. Hearing something off to the side, he stopped, and Brutus came to attention. "Right? I heard it too. Not sure what's going on out there, buddy, but it doesn't feel right, does it?"

Walton slipped into the trees and out of sight, with Brutus tucked up close beside him. The dog didn't trust those noises but was not worried, yet curious and interested in this new game they were playing. So Brutus wasn't turned on in terms of war training. He wasn't sensing danger the way Walton was.

Stilled, he rested behind the tree and waited to see what would flush out of the bushes first. When nothing happened, Brutus shifted uneasily, and Walton placed a hand on his shoulder, reassuring him. They needed to wait. Something was going on, and Walton couldn't tell exactly *what* just yet. So no way he would rush it.

After another long moment, he sensed movement off to the left. With that forewarning, he watched as Hawk stepped out from behind the trees, with a gun in his hand. Not a hunting rifle but a small handgun. He didn't approach them though. He seemed confused as to which way to go. Walton realized that Hawk was turned around and had no clue where the lodge was.

As Walton continued to watch Hawk, he shifted uneasily, more unnerved about being alone out here, with good reason. A hell of a lot of things could go wrong. It was really not smart to get lost or to get too far away from where you were expected to be.

Hearing voices in the distance, Walton remained blended into the background, as the others called out for Hawk.

"Where the hell are you, dude?"

"I'm over here."

They burst through the brush, laughing and joking when they saw him. "What the hell, man?"

Hawk shrugged. "I have to admit that I lost my bearings out here."

"You don't want to fucking do that," Chad stated, with a headshake. "It's way too easy to get lost out here. We've got to stay together."

"That might be true," Hawk conceded, "but I thought I heard something."

"Like what?" Chad asked.

"Probably that fucking dog of yours."

"It's not my dog, apparently," Chad snapped, with an eye roll.

The other men didn't say anything about that. They just waited and watched, as if every word had to be measured and weighed. Nobody quite knew which way people would react now, and it was a hell of an uneasy situation for supposed friends to be in.

Walton watched from a distance, his hand on Brutus, when once again an argument broke out among the four guys. This time Walton didn't hear what started it, but he felt it had to do with the War Dog. Once again, Chad stormed off toward the lodge. At least he seemed to keep his bearings.

"Come on. Let's go," Darren said, urging Hawk to pick up the pace. "Last thing we want to do is lose our bearings out there. Chad might be an asshole, but the one thing he can do is navigate."

Hawk snorted. "He's the one who told me to come over

here."

The threesome unknowingly traipsed past Walton, heading toward the lodge once again.

Hawk added, "I just want some bloody breakfast, and how about we leave early? I really don't want to be around here anymore."

As their voices disappeared in front of him, Walton relaxed ever-so-slightly. Just as he was ready to head toward the lodge himself, he heard a gunshot, followed by a second one. With Brutus at his heels, the two of them ran toward the sounds.

As soon as they broke through the brush and into a clearing, Walton figured he was maybe one-quarter mile away from the lodge. All four hunters were up ahead, except Chad was on the ground, with a head wound bleeding profusely. As Walton burst through the trees, the three men standing just stared at him, then down at their friend. Soon Rick appeared coming from the lodge toward them too.

"We didn't shoot him," Darren yelled hysterically. "Honest to God. I swear. … I just arrived, and … we got separated again. Chad took off, ran ahead of us, and then, as we came here, we found him like this." He turned to the others. "Right? I didn't shoot him."

"I didn't shoot him either," Hawk said nervously. "Jesus, we were getting lost again, so we came bolting forward."

"Were you guys all in each other's sight the entire time?" Walton asked, his gaze going from one to the other.

They all looked at each other and shrugged. Hawk replied, "More or less, but, we were running forward, so I wasn't looking behind me to see if they were following. We were all running to catch up with Chad," Hawk explained. "We all went through the trees. It's dark as hell in that forest."

"Were you all going at the same speed?" Walton asked.

Hawk frowned at him. "Man, do you really think one of us killed Chad?"

"I don't know what I think," Walton admitted, as he knelt down and checked on Chad. "But I heard two shots, and I see both hit Chad's head, fired at close range. ... This was no accident."

"It could have been an accident," said George, the one who rarely spoke.

"No," Walton countered, turning to him. "This was no accident. I don't know if you've got another friend out here, but, if not, I'm betting that one of you three just killed a second one of your friends. What do you want to bet it was the same guy who killed the first one?" At that, they all stared at him, completely dumbstruck, as silence fell all around them. Walton nodded once. "So, nobody is leaving until I get the cops up here." Walton had his phone out, dialing 9-1-1.

"Cops? ... They'll never come out here," George declared, "and don't ask me how I know."

"You should know," Hawk stated, frowning at him, "since you were a cop."

At that news. Walton spun around and asked, "Why aren't you a cop anymore?"

The other two men snorted. "Because apparently Georgie here is a bad cop. He got kicked off the force because of it, but he still knows his shit."

George spun on his friends. "Shut the fuck up," he yelled. "I didn't have anything to do with shooting Chad, and you don't get to blame it on me."

"Maybe we should be blaming Rudy's death on you,"

Hawk suggested menacingly. "Maybe you killed Rudy too."

"I didn't fucking kill anybody," George spat, an expression of disbelief taking over his face. He looked genuinely flushed, but that could be due to anything. "Do you guys even hear yourselves?"

"Yeah, three of us are here now, where there used to be four," Hawk pointed out, staring at George. "When I came upon this scene, I saw Chad on the ground, and *you* were kneeling at his side."

"Yeah, I came upon him first because I was right behind him, remember? I was ahead of you. I didn't kill him," George declared, staring at them in shock. "I can't believe you would even say that."

"After two of our friends have been killed, of course I would say that," Hawk stated.

"I didn't kill him," George repeated. "The last thing I want is anybody here accusing me of that. If this K9 guy gets the cops in here, you know that they'll look at *all* of us *all* over again. And that's something not a one of us can handle."

And, with that, complete silence fell for maybe a full minute, before Rick yelled, "What the hell happened?"

Walton looked up at him. "One of these three just popped another one of their friends." Then he faced the so-called group of hunters and friends. "With the friends you guys have," Walton began, unsure of how to handle this mess, "you may want to get new ones."

CHAPTER 9

CHELSEA COULDN'T BELIEVE it. She'd heard the story several times, and it was still mind-boggling. She was huddled in the kitchen beside Julie, the two of them silent, just as silent as everybody else in the lodge, as they waited for the cops to arrive. It wasn't a good day. As a matter of fact, it was a shitty day. They had decided to leave the body exactly where it was, but, with one man standing guard on it, just in case forensics needed some civilian chain of custody in force.

That had been Rick's idea. It wasn't something that the others were prepared to argue about, and nobody really wanted to touch the body as it was.

As for Walton, he thought that was a good idea to keep the wild animals off Chad's body, since they couldn't move the body until forensics got here. So Rick used his satellite phone to call his ranch hand out there to take a shift to guard the body.

When Walton was asked to explain further, he just smiled at Chelsea. "Nobody will confess as to who was there first, and nobody who was there first will confess to it either. Although George admitted to being right behind Chad but swears he had nothing to do with it so says he wasn't there first as the killer would have been and that's not him."

"Of course not," she muttered. "This is just unbelievable." She glanced over worriedly as Rick walked into the room, slipped an arm around his wife's shoulders, and just held her.

Walton gave Chelsea a quick hug too. "It'll be okay."

She looked up at him and nodded, but the start of real fear formed deep inside her. "Do you really think they shot their own friend?"

"After hearing of the earlier death of their other friend Rudy, that's certainly a good working theory," Walton noted. "Can you think of any other reason why somebody would shoot Chad?"

"Other than being an asshole and a bully and a misogynist, no," Chelsea replied. "I mean, he came up here to my brother's lodge out in the middle of nowhere … but why?" she asked. "Outside of the War Dog getting out and about, and Chad's messed-up hunting fun, … what was Chad's purpose in coming up here?"

"From what I overheard when the guys were up on the ledge, Chad wanted to get to the bottom of whoever had shot Rudy," Walton shared, shaking his head. "That's what everything leads back to."

Chelsea nodded. "So whoever shot the first one may have wanted to silence Chad, particularly if he was getting close to sorting it out."

"Or," Rick interjected, looking at Walton for the tenth time, "even Chad's own crew was fed up and tired of him and shot him. His death surely wasn't accidental," he declared.

Walton nodded. "Close range, two shots to the head, from the back. Either somebody Chad trusted was walking right behind him or somebody else snuck up behind Chad and popped him. Now, you may already know this, Rick, but just to be clear, you and I will both end up under suspicion, since we both arrived at the crime scene so quickly."

"Shit." Rick frowned and rubbed his temples.

Julie grabbed his hand. "You didn't do anything, so nothing to worry about."

He gave her a wry look. "It would be nice if I believed that, but I don't really."

"Will the police find something they don't like when they look into your history?" Walton asked Rick. "Because now's a really good time to bring that out in the open."

Rick shook his head. "No, I don't have any big scary secrets." He hung his head, sighing. "I know it sounds selfish as hell, but my concern is my business. It's one thing to weather a lack of guests and even some shitty guests," he shared, "but it's another thing to weather a murder."

"But it's not your fault," Chelsea pointed out. "You had nothing to do with it. I know that Julie was in the kitchen and you and I were on the veranda when we heard the two shots."

"Yet," Rick added, "but since we're husband and wife and you're my sister, somebody's just as likely to say that our alibis are no good either."

"That goes for all of us," Walton pointed out.

"You at least have a good reason for being here," George said, as the rest of Chad's friends stepped into the kitchen. An odd expression was on George's face.

"K9 guy also could have shot Chad," Darren suggested. "I mean, he wanted the dog."

"You're forgetting something," Rick pointed out. "He already got the dog from Chad yesterday."

Darren's shoulders slumped. "Yeah, I guess so. ... It still sucks though."

Rick repeated, "Walton didn't have anything to do with it."

Darren replied, "*I* didn't have anything to do with the first death and now look at this—a second one. Shit."

"If you didn't shoot Chad," Walton said, turning to face him, "then you must have a pretty good idea which of the other two could have done it. Because if one was with you, running through the woods, where was the other one?"

Darren looked at him and shrugged. "We all split up because it's so thick with the trees back there. I heard their movements, but I couldn't really see anybody. You know what it's like out there. Tons of shrubbery and tons of brush amid tons of big-ass trees that cut out all the sunlight. So, if Chad was just standing there, somebody could have walked up, popped him, dashed back into the woods, then raced back out again to make it appear that he was the one who found him."

"*Great*," Hawk snapped. "So, let's see, … you're putting that on me then."

Darren shrugged. "I'm just saying it's a possibility."

"It's not a fucking possibility that I shot Chad," Hawk swore and looked over at George. "Where the hell were you when all this chaos was going on?"

"Running," he stated, "particularly once I heard the shots."

"*Right*," Hawk replied, "but did anybody see you?"

"What the hell, man? You're trying to put this on me?"

"It's not a matter of putting it on you. It's a matter of figuring out where everybody was at the time," Hawk explained. "All I know is that *I* didn't shoot Chad."

Chelsea's gaze went from one to the other. It was so hard to even contemplate that anybody would want to kill someone. Chad was an asshole, no doubt, but he was also supposedly their friend. "Could somebody else be out there?"

Rick looked over at her and shook his head. "That's always a possibility, but it's just not very likely. In this weather, camping outside with the elements and the wildlife …"

"But it is possible?" Chad's crew asked, practically in unison.

"I mean, other places, other lodges, other cabins must be around here." Hawk looked at Rick expectantly.

"Not for a hell of a long way from here," Rick stated, facing them. "You know how far off the beaten path my lodge is. And my property entails a lot of acres. We're out here for a reason, and it's called privacy."

"Privacy is one thing, until people start dying, and then it's a whole different story," Hawk muttered begrudgingly.

Rick smirked. "You also know as well as I do that the privacy is still one of the big pulls for my guests. You guys came up here looking to find some privacy yourselves, to get away from it all, to get away from the cops and their innuendoes. To get away from all that nastiness of Rudy's death."

The three men nodded. "But we didn't expect Chad to die in the process," Darren noted. "You sure he was shot in the *back* of his head?" he asked hopefully.

"Didn't you look at him?" Hawk asked, turning on him.

"No, I didn't look at him," Darren confirmed, hanging his head, his eyes bloodshot. "Jesus, I can't stand the sight of blood. … You know that."

Hawk snorted. "That is true. Darren will pass out at the slightest provocation."

"No need to be judgmental about it," Darren grumbled.

"I can't do needles either, and it's not my fault, so whatever."

But Hawk turned to Walton and added, "He really doesn't do well with blood."

Walton didn't say anything to that comment. If you shot somebody from the back, that shooter may not need to ensure the guy was dead. If you wanted confirmation, you would shoot him in the front of the head. Walton studied Darren. "What was your question about the shooting though? Why did you ask that about where the shots came from?"

"I know it's stupid, but I just wondered if, … if maybe Chad could have done it to himself."

"If the shots had been from the front or the side or any other angle, maybe," Walton replied. "But not this time. Whoever shot Chad came up behind him and popped him in the back of the head twice. Chad couldn't have done it himself, and the other thing is, … no way Chad could have fired the second shot."

"Well, shit," Darren muttered, as he slumped in place. "That cancels that theory."

Walton nodded. "It does, and, yeah, I did contemplate suicide for all of a half second, until I saw the body. After that, just no need to contemplate anything but murder." Walton sighed. "Unfortunately Chad bled out and was dead pretty fast."

"Unfortunately?" One of the men turned and glared at him.

"A figure of speech," Walton replied. "All I'm saying is that he didn't shoot himself. That would have been anatomically impossible. And, if you wanted to make it look like that, you failed."

The men just stared at him. "You really don't like us, do

you?"

"Should I? You were all a part of that whole craziness with the War Dog and Rudy's death," Walton pointed out. "So, I don't know whether you really had anything to do with Chad's murder or not. You say you didn't, and I'm more than prepared to believe that," he shared. "I've got bigger things on my plate right now. Yet I don't understand what happened to your first friend. Now all of a sudden, we have a second dead friend, and that is beyond concerning. Would you have believed this yourself?"

"No, … you're not kidding," Hawk muttered. "And, if you continue along that line, you've got to wonder if the rest of us aren't in more danger."

"What are you talking about?" Darren asked, looking at Hawk in confusion.

"Just think about it. Two of us are dead. What are the chances that it's supposed to end up with three more of us dead?"

Darren's eyebrows shot up, and he looked at Hawk in horror. "Then that would mean that either you or George here are still planning to kill me."

Hawk clarified, "Or some unknown third party. That's exactly what I'm saying, and we don't know for sure that it isn't the case."

"Crap," Darren muttered. "You know I really don't want to hear that, right?"

His buddy nodded. "None of us want to. This isn't how we thought this would go down. We came up here to let off a little steam, to ease up some of the stress of having the cops looking at us. And honestly, because Chad was putting the pressure on us too. All we've got now is more cops looking at us," Hawk pointed out. "So how the hell does that work for us?"

"Not very well," Darren stated uneasily, "and that's part of the problem."

"So, then I have to wonder," Walton noted, eyeing them, "is there any chance that this is all by grand design?"

"What do you mean?" Hawk asked, turning to him.

"Think about it. You're now wondering if one of your other two friends is out to kill you. And, if that were the case, this isn't random. Somebody doesn't just decide one day that his friends suck and that he needs to kill them. So, what could possibly explain anybody wanting to take you three out? Maybe somebody took out the first two, thinking the other three would get paranoid and take each other out. Or maybe some unknown person plans to take out all five of you? I know you probably don't want me asking questions, but, when the cops arrive, they'll be asking plenty of questions of their own."

"Well, shit," Hawk groaned, staring at him. "I don't even know what to say to that."

"How about the truth?" Walton asked. "That would be a great place to start."

"We're really not hiding anything. You have to know that. We came up here because, ... because of Chad." Hawk stopped, shook his head, "Chad wanted us to go off and have a weekend together, get rid of all the stress that we've been under. It's really not rocket science. We weren't planning anything."

"Yet you didn't want to come? Any of you? Except for maybe Chad."

"No, I didn't want to come at all, and I told Chad that too," Hawk proclaimed, shaking his head.

"But he didn't get it?" Walton asked.

"No, he didn't get it. Chad didn't see why I wasn't ready to come have a weekend with *the bros*."

Darren turned and looked at him. "Why didn't you want a weekend with us?"

"For the same reason you didn't," Hawk declared. "It's a stupid idea. I don't know who killed Rudy, and I don't want anybody looking at me for it. Just the thought that somebody might even be thinking that it's us, as a group, killing off our friends is bizarre. I mean, thinking just one of us wanted to kill Rudy is bad enough, but all of us coming together to plan Rudy's murder? It just … didn't sit right."

Darren nodded. "My fiancée was really having a shit fit about this trip too. But I didn't say that to Chad because I knew he would have a freaking meltdown over it."

A snort of laughter came from Hawk. "Yeah, he would have. He was against all women in a big way."

"Why is that?" Chelsea asked.

Hawk turned to her, then shrugged. "Chad's wife, … she left him, took his kids, and took all his money."

"So, all women are shits then because of the actions of one woman, is that it?" Chelsea asked, shaking her head.

Hawk shrugged and nodded. "Pretty much, and you can't really blame the guy for thinking that he got the raw deal because he really did. He lost everything."

"Did anybody look at why she may have taken off?" Chelsea asked, her tone hardening.

"Nope, we didn't, and believe me that Chad wouldn't have cared either. He considered her leaving him as a betrayal, and, if a betrayal to him, it was a betrayal to us."

"So, it comes down to a *bros* thing again," Chelsea noted.

Hawk considered it and then nodded. "Maybe, … but

we didn't think of it that way. It was just a matter of loyalty. Somebody did Chad wrong, and we were really pissed and sorry about it, … for him."

"Did anybody do anything about his wife?" Chelsea asked the group. "Did anybody talk to her? Did anybody hurt her, beat her up, or do anything to her?"

"No, of course not," Hawk declared, an angry expression on his face. "What the hell kind of people do you think we are?" Then he winced. "Shit. I guess from your perspective, we're nothing but a group of angry men, killing each other off." He hung his head. "We're not like that. I admit we probably didn't give a great first impression because … Chad somehow—and I don't quite understand this—controlled us, all of us. I, for one, am a little ashamed of that."

Groaning, Hawk rubbed his head and then continued. "I know it makes no sense. It really doesn't. I don't know why Chad had that level of control over us, but it was really hard to shake him when he got into that mood, wasn't it?" He turned to his buddies.

They both nodded. "Honestly, none of us wanted to come up here," Darren admitted.

Chelsea looked over at the three men. "Then why did you?"

Hawk shrugged. "Because of that worry, that suspicion that somebody in our group *did* kill Rudy," he shared. "I wanted to know more about it. I wanted to know what the hell was going on, but *this* is not what I expected." He stared off into the distance. "Honest to God, I didn't want the cops looking into my business. … Now I'm not bad or anything, but we do a bunch of recreational drugs."

He flushed but kept going. "That's a problem. We all do it. None of us are really hiding it, but we don't want the cops poking around and making our lives miserable about it. It's not that big of a deal to us, but having the cops around gets us in shit with our partners and, in my case, also with my family, and I really can't afford that."

"Crap," George muttered. "They'll really dig all through that, won't they?"

"They won't if you just tell them up front," Walton suggested. "If it's recreational drugs, and you're fessing up, it's hardly worth bothering with. Murder trumps everything else. But you already have a bad rep with the cops, don't you?"

"I do," George confirmed, "and I'm not proud of that either."

"Did it have anything to do with any of the other guys here?"

George shook his head. "No, it really didn't. It was all about my former profession, being a cop. I took bribes, stole evidence as a cop on the payroll. So I lost my job. I can never be a cop again. It was a stupid thing on my part, and I've been paying for it ever since."

Walton sighed. "Stupid is as stupid does, and it happens to a lot of people. It happens to all of us at one point or another. We're not exactly getting anywhere here, but you'll all need to line up your positions on a map," Walton suggested, "particularly in reference to Chad's body."

"Yeah, well, that ain't happening. What you've also got to know," George added, looking at Walton, "is that only one of us could find our way out in the woods, and that was Chad."

Hawk and Darren nodded. "Yeah, Chad was the navigator, more or less. That's one of the good things about him. Otherwise we were always lost. Still, Chad's the one who somehow managed to get us home, which is great, but it also sucks. Whenever we went out, we were stuck with whatever time frame Chad had in mind."

"Interesting," Walton murmured.

Darren replied, "*Interesting* for you maybe, but not so much for us. Honestly, we just want to go home at this point."

Walton nodded. "That's a good idea, but you can't go home before the cops get here and talk to you."

"But you can't hold us here, can you?" Hawk asked.

"I could. I could make a citizen's arrest and really make you all miserable. That would be a shame." The men stopped and stared at Walton. He shrugged. "Believe me that I'm not here to make your life miserable. I think you've probably got enough of that coming up without getting more from me."

"What do you mean?" Hawk asked, frowning at him.

"The cops will connect Chad's death right back to Rudy's murder," Walton explained. "Absolutely no way they won't. You're just trying to ignore the elephant in the room, but it won't work, and you know that."

"He's right," George muttered.

"You're the ex-cop, so you should know," Darren shot back to him.

George scrubbed his face. "They will. The cops will look at this and see it as being completely related, and we won't get off easy on any of it. ... Shit, I knew I shouldn't have come on this damn trip."

"So why did you?" Chelsea asked.

"Honestly? Curiosity and a little bit of fear. I've got some issues that Chad knows about, and he threatened to tell people, getting me into a whole lot more trouble."

"He blackmailed you?" Chelsea asked in disbelief. "This

is the man you call a friend?"

George shrugged. "Yeah, I know it sounds stupid, but, up until now, I would have said he was a friend."

"*Great*. Did you ever consider getting new friends?" Chelsea asked, shaking her head.

"Have to now," George grumbled. "They're dying left, right, and center, like flies and shit." And, with that, he got up and announced, "I'm going upstairs. I'm a little wrecked over all this. I just want a break and some time to think about what the hell's going on in my world."

"You do that," Walton said. "The cops should be here in a few hours."

"*Great*," George muttered, "just what I wanted." And, with that, he headed to the stairs and walked up to the second floor. The others watched as he left and then turned back to Walton.

"We didn't do it, you know?" Hawk stated.

"I hope not," Walton replied, "but, even though Chad was a bully and an asshole, I still think your friend deserved more than to be shot from behind out in the middle of nowhere."

Hawk and Darren winced. "That just isn't anything we would do."

Walton nodded. "You can say that until you're blue in the face, but the reality is that somebody did do it, and you guys just haven't figured out who—which is beyond important at this stage. So you guys need to sit down and, to the best of your ability, sketch out a map, showing exactly where you were when Chad was killed. Share that so we all know, and then we'll go from there."

Chelsea caught the note of amusement in his tone.

"And yet," Darren replied, glaring at him, "this really has

nothing to do with you."

"Maybe not, unless I'm on the hit list now too," he noted, as a warning heated up in his tone. "So, if you think you're leaving right now because the cops are coming to investigate, think again. I will stop you."

The two men stiffened. "So, you really don't believe us, do you?"

"I'm not sure what I believe at this point," Walton admitted, "but what I can tell you is that somebody who was a troublemaker and a liar and a bully is dead. He was your friend, and he was out hunting with you guys. So, tell me where in all of this I'm supposed to trust any of you or automatically believe anything you have to say."

They just looked at him, then at each other. "So we can go to our rooms then?" Darren asked in a hard, mocking tone.

"Yeah, I think you can go to your rooms." Walton nodded. "It's not as if you'll leave the lodge without anybody knowing."

"Really?" Darren asked. "What will you do? Stay up all night?"

"I don't have to," he declared, and he snapped his fingers.

Immediately Brutus stood at attention, his ears forward, and, with a silent hand command that Chelsea barely saw, Brutus bared his teeth and growled at them.

WALTON SMIRKED AS Darren and Hawk just stared at Walton and the War Dog. The two hunters visibly tensed up and then nodded, almost in a sign of defeat.

"*Great*, so we're not going anywhere until morning," Darren conceded.

"If the cops allow you to," Walton muttered. "And let's hope none of the rest of us get murdered in our beds overnight. In fact, I would suggest that you three sleep in the same room for just that reason." The two men on their way out of the room stopped and looked at him. Walton shrugged. "If there are three of you gathered together, it will be harder for one of you to kill the others. I would like to think that at least one of you would wake up, if you're under attack again."

They looked at each other, then at Walton. Hawk asked, "But what if we're drugged?"

Walton frowned. "So we're not talking marijuana now, are we? Chad brought drugs with him, like a date rape drug? Is that something that your friends know how to use?"

"I have no idea," Hawk replied in frustration. "I didn't have anything to do with this shit."

"But according to everybody else in your group, neither did they," Walton stated, eyeing him carefully. "All I'm saying is that all of us need to be on guard."

"Yeah, *great*," Hawk muttered, rubbing his temples. "Yet I do appreciate the warning." And, with that, he turned and walked out of the room.

Darren frowned at Walton. "You really mean it, don't you?"

Walton nodded. "You only have to look at the odds," he pointed out. "I'm not a betting man. How about you?"

He swallowed and shook his head. "No, I just want to go home to my girlfriend, man. We're engaged, and I promised Elena that I would come back, whole and healthy."

"The fact that you even had to promise that says something." Walton pointed out.

"Yeah, it says that she's a hell of a lot smarter than I am. She told me not to go. She said that Chad was on a downward slope and that he was angry, so I needed to stay away from him, but I didn't listen. Chad's been my buddy for a long time, but she hasn't known him all that long, and I thought she couldn't really know anything about him. Still, she nailed it. She nailed it after just a few minutes of talking to the damn bastard, and I'm the idiot who didn't listen." And, with that, Darren turned and walked out.

As soon as the other men were safely out of earshot, Walton turned to Rick. "We need to bring the body here."

He nodded. "I was hoping you would say that. I really didn't want to spend the night on guard out there, and we need to relieve my ranch hand. Plus, I don't know how long it will be until the cops get here. Have you got another reason?"

"Yeah, I didn't get a chance to search him," Walton shared, his tone hard. He stood up, looked at the women, and added, "I can go alone, but I could use his help."

"Go," Julie prompted. Then she hesitated and added, "I presume you're taking Brutus?"

"I am taking the dog," he confirmed, "and Rick will need to bring a rifle, given this is a hell of a sticky situation for all of us. You women need a gun apiece as well. Plus, stay together until one of us returns."

They both nodded.

Rick got up and grabbed a hunting rifle and two pistols. He gave the handguns to Julie and Chelsea. With nods shared to all, the men headed outside. "How do you plan to carry him back?" Rick asked.

Walton shrugged. "We can make a pallet and take turns

pulling him home."

Rick asked, "What about storing him? I don't have a place to put him."

"I know," Walton agreed. "I already checked your commercial freezer."

"Yeah, and we don't have a huge walk-in cooler or anything. It's not as if this is a place where we can store bodies."

"But you do store meat."

Rick stared at him and nodded. "Yes, we do have a hanging place, but that's hardly respectful."

"I get it, and obviously it's not where we want to put Chad, if we had any other place to preserve his body. Not to mention the fact that it's like hanging a hunting trophy."

Rick nodded. "Where do you want to put him then?"

"In the back of a police car and be rid of him."

Rick hesitated. "You really think one of these guys shot Chad, don't you?"

"Yeah, I sure do," Walton shared, "but, for the life of me, I'm stuck between two of them."

Rick stared at him. "You're ahead of me. I can't figure if any of these three can be trusted."

"Oh, ... I'm not talking about trust," Walton pointed out, "because I don't think that even enters into it. However, I do think there's more to this than we know."

"Of course there is," Rick muttered. "The trick is trying to get anybody to give a shit about dealing with it."

They walked out to the body, where Rick's one and only ranch employee was sitting, having a smoke. As they approached, he hopped up. "Are the cops here?"

"Not yet."

"Well, damn, I was really hoping to go back inside and get some food." He glanced nervously around.

"Anybody been out here?" Walton asked.

He looked at them and shook his head. "Ain't nobody else here."

"Maybe, maybe not," Rick muttered and released the ranch hand to return to the lodge. Rick turned and asked Walton, "What now?"

"Now I search the body. I need a witness. That would really help if you say I didn't or did find something here. Plus, film it too. We need both."

"In that case, go ahead," Rick noted. "I don't want to touch him." Rick pulled out his phone and switched on the camera app.

"Right, and with good reason," Walton said. "I'm not sure what the hell's going on, but something definitely is off about all this." He approached the dead body and squatted beside Chad, then quickly checked his pockets. The pockets yielded a cell phone, which was also something Walton needed to go through, but he found nothing else except a wallet. He flipped open the wallet, looked through it, and then whistled. "This guy's got multiple IDs in here."

"Really?" Rick asked, coming over and taking a look, filming all the while. "Why the hell does he have all that?"

"I don't know, unless he was planning to take off, which could be plan B, considering Chad was potentially looking at a murder charge or was being investigated for that and more. Still," Walton added in confusion, "it's not as if he needs multiple IDs for that."

"Yes, but, once your passport is triggered at the airport, the authorities know where you're going. If they can, they'll stop you before you get on the plane. If you're already on the plane, and it's still on the tarmac, they'll haul you off of it."

"I guess," Walton replied doubtfully. "It just doesn't

seem like something Chad would do."

"Why not?" Rick asked, turning to him.

Walton shrugged. "Chad honestly didn't seem all that brilliant."

Rick chuckled. "I'm not arguing with that. He definitely didn't come across as the brainy type. He was all brawn."

"Yep, he sure as hell was. Yet I've met a lot of strange people. Do you have much trouble up here?"

"No, I wouldn't say so, at least we haven't had much trouble. I hope this isn't the start of something we really don't want to continue."

"Of course not," Walton murmured, as he continued to go through Chad's pockets.

When Walton got down to checking the pant legs, Rick gulped, a hint of repulsion in his tone. "Are you seriously checking his pant legs?"

"Yes, I'm seriously checking his pant legs." Then he smiled and turned to Rick. "And it's a good thing I did."

"Why is that?" he asked, frowning.

"You got the video still recording, right?" Rick nodded. "Good thing you're filming it all, so keep that on." Then he held up the item Walton had fished out of an ankle holster under his pants.

"A hunting knife?"

"Yep," Walton stated. "It doesn't really help when you are facing a loaded gun, but I'm really hoping one of his buddies can tell us what they think about this."

"You expect them to?"

"Yeah, I expect them to because it'll be one of the reasons they don't go down for murder, and, right now, we've got *two* murders. I don't think one of them wants anything to do with this."

"What about the other two?" Rick challenged.

"I think they probably had something to do with it."

"Two of them?" Rick asked, staring at Walton in disbelief.

"Yeah, it's the only way they can cover their alibis."

"Oh, shit," Rick muttered, staring at him, nonplussed. "I hadn't considered that."

Walton nodded. "Hopefully it won't be something that we have to continue to consider, but knowing that something shifty is going on here and that two men are dead now, it's not something we can leave to chance."

He kept searching the body, and, when he got down to Chad's boots and socks, Walton nodded. "This is what I was looking for." And, with that, he pulled out a small USB key. He looked back over at Rick and asked, "What do you want to bet this is the reason that Chad was killed?"

CHAPTER 10

CHELSEA HAD BEEN so happy when the guys safely returned to the lodge. She and Julie had remained together, each of them armed, during their absence. Walton told her to go to bed and to get some sleep, and he would fill her in tomorrow. She did manage to sleep and was awoken by the arrival of the police. She bolted out of bed, noted it was still pitch-black outside, got dressed, and headed downstairs. She wanted to be in the middle of whatever this was, if only to ensure that she could find a way past it and the nightmares later. As she walked into the living room, rubbing her eyes, she felt a hand on her shoulder and turned to see Walton, smiling at her.

She opened her arms and wrapped him up in a big hug. He hugged her back, and that alone gave her such a sense of peace and contentedness. She looked up at him and smiled. "You're a good hugger." When his eyebrows shot up, she realized how little experience he had at getting compliments and how utterly unfamiliar he was with the idea. "I mean it," she said, as she slipped out of his arms slightly to turn and look back at the front doors. "I gather the police are here?"

"Yes, I was gonna tell you, but you didn't need to get up."

"But I do," she stated. "I don't want this rolling around in my brain, causing me nightmares. I'm much better off to just see what is going on and to go from there."

"Fine," he muttered. "The cops are out now with Rick. He was guarding the body."

"Not you?" she asked. He shook his head. "Any particular reason? You generally don't let go so easily."

He smiled, realizing that she knew him pretty well, and wondered why she was so observant where he was concerned. "I wanted to see if the men would still be here."

"Ah." Chelsea nodded. "So you're trying to keep an eye on them."

"I am. There are still three of them, and I'm just not comfortable with you and Julie being here with them," he shared.

"Do you really think we're in danger?" Julie asked, coming up behind them.

He winced, and Chelsea pinched him. "Now you've got her all worried."

"It's just a matter of being cautious."

Chelsea searched his face for a long moment and then nodded. "I guess that makes sense. We already have somebody who's been murdered, so let's hope there won't be a third."

"Exactly," Walton agreed. "Not only let there *not* be a third body, but we have to consider the fact that whatever is going on happened long before these guys ever got here to the lodge. We are not all that important to them, just witnesses to be silenced," he explained, "and they will make that clear fairly quickly."

"Ah, so we're expendable? Is that what you're saying?" Chelsea asked.

He hesitated, then shrugged. "It is one way to look at it."

"It seems to me that's the *only* way to look at it," Chelsea

declared, worry etched on her face. "It's not a very comfortable idea either."

"Of course not," Walton muttered. "I was trying not to
upset you or Julie."

Julie frowned, hugging herself.

Chelsea gave him a wry smile. "I thank you for that, but
I would rather be in the know and, if I need to be extra
careful, then I will be."

"Then be extra careful," he stated. "You both need to be.
Even with Rick and me in the house or nearby, keep those
guns on you."

Julie nodded, exchanging glances with Chelsea, then
announced, "On that note, I'll go to the kitchen and put on
coffee." She looked outside in the still-dark world around
them. "Any idea how long the cops will be?"

"We ended up leaving the body out there," Walton
shared, "so they'll check the area and then bring it back to
the lodge."

"We don't have a place to store it," Julie noted worriedly.

"Nobody will have to store it. I'm guessing they'll take it
back with them," Walton shared. "At least they should. They
knew a body was here, so they should have come prepared to
deal with it."

"All these *should haves* make me a little concerned," Julie
pointed out. "What are the odds that they'll have a body bag
or whatever?"

"They will," Walton said, with a smile. "That is pretty
standard protocol when this happens."

Julie nodded, but it was obvious that she was more worried about everything else than hearing what he had to say.

"Any chance of getting some coffee?" he asked, reminding her.

She smiled and said, "Coming right up," and she quickly disappeared into the kitchen.

"You're very good with her," Chelsea told him, smiling.

He intentionally had been gentle with Julie. "She is pregnant, worried about her child, and has all this stress she's been under. Plus, Julie really wants people to be gentle with each other," he noted, "and I understand that she's really struggling with all this, but she's doing a fine job."

"She is, and, of course, … being pregnant has made her all the more nervous, though she tries not to show it."

"Of course," he agreed. "It's not exactly the start of her pregnancy that she was hoping for, and it makes me wonder if Rick might just shut down the business for the next little bit."

Hearing more voices, he wrapped an arm around Chelsea's shoulders. With her tucked up against him, he stepped outside onto the front porch.

"Is that to let the police know that I'm not involved?" she asked, with an attempt at humor in her tone, but it fell flat when she watched the men carrying the body between them. "Well, Jesus," she muttered, as she hurriedly buried her face in Walton's shoulder.

He just held her tight. When she did look back up again, the cops were at the back of one of the two police vehicles. "They'll just take it away like that?" she asked.

"Yes," he murmured, "that would make sense."

"Sure, it would," she muttered, then shook her head. "*Not.* Nothing about this makes sense." He squeezed her shoulders again, and she realized just how natural it felt to be here with him. "Hell, we shouldn't even be here. If only you had come back for your extra sessions."

"I was planning on it," he replied. "I was also trying to get into a little bit better shape."

"Why? So you could show off?"

He looked at her in surprise and then grinned. "Maybe."

"*Maybe*," she muttered. "You do know that I've seen you at your worst, right?"

"I know. I just thought it might be nice if you saw me at my best."

She stilled, then looked up at him and asked, amusement in her tone, "Is that important?"

"It seemed to be at the time," he noted, glancing down at her. "Yet it pales in comparison to all this."

"Maybe," she agreed, "but it also helps me to understand how your mind works."

"I'm pretty sure you have a good idea how my mind works already," he admitted, with a chuckle.

"I don't know," she teased. "Weird and wacky things go on in that head of yours." She tapped it gently.

Just then the police officers walked over. Walton quickly introduced Chelsea to them. They just nodded, tilted their hats. "Ma'am."

She smiled and said, "I can't tell you how happy I am that you're here."

The detectives nodded. "I'm Detective McKenna and this is my partner, Detective Hogan. Ugly business going on here."

"Ugly business for all of us," she noted. "Not what we thought would happen when we came up here."

"Yet you came up after a War Dog, I hear," the lead detective mentioned.

"He did," Chelsea said, pointing Walton's way, "and this is my brother's place, so I came up with Walton."

"Ah," the detective replied, as if that made all the difference in the world. He looked over at Walton and said, "I guess we need to talk."

Walton nodded. "Rick has already offered you the use of his office, so we can go in there, where it's private."

Rick hesitated and then asked, "Should I come too?"

The detective shook his head. "No, this will be just the two of us." And, with that, he motioned at Walton, and he walked ahead into the lodge to reach the office.

The other detective stayed behind. "Maybe you can give me your version of events."

Chelsea raised her eyebrows. "Sure, whatever events I can help you with, I'm happy to, but I wasn't out there when they found the body." She answered every question he had to the best of her ability. When he finally ran down, she was almost shaking. She looked over at her brother and said, "I'll go into the kitchen and grab a cup of coffee."

"You do that, and check on Julie, would you?"

With a nod, Chelsea quickly made her escape. In the kitchen, she found Julie busy cooking. "Cooking?"

"Dumb, I know, but I'm really struggling with how I'm supposed to handle all this. So I'm doing anything I can to keep busy."

"That's a good idea," she muttered. "I wish I had something to keep me busy."

"You can always help me in the kitchen. After all, *that's where women belong*," she quipped, with an eye roll.

"Did they actually say that to you?"

"Of course, and I don't know whether Chad and his group meant it, or it was a joke," she noted. "We get all kinds of jokesters up here, and that's a fairly common topic."

"Yeah, I bet that gets old very quickly," Chelsea muttered.

"It sure does," Julie agreed, with a laugh, "but that's all right, as this too shall pass." And, with that, she motioned at Chelsea. "These need to be rolled into balls before we can get them into the oven."

"I'm on it," Chelsea replied.

And, with that, the two of them buckled down and, before long, had some mini breakfast crepes made and also some cookies and granola bars.

"Do you just keep these recipes in your head?" Chelsea asked curiously.

Julie smiled at her. "Guests are typically only here for a few days, so it's pretty easy to use the same recipes. Once I found a dozen that worked, I've just stuck with them."

"That makes sense," Chelsea noted. "Doing the same recipes is probably easier to plan for and all."

"Exactly," Julie confirmed. "It made my life easier and helps me with the grocery list, once I figure out what I need. Some of these keep a really long time too, and they're also easy for the men to take out on a hunting trip," she explained, "so it just works all around. And I can always do something different if I feel like it, but I know I'm prepared for the basics."

As they kept themselves busy, Chelsea asked Julie about the baby. "You never did give me a due date."

"No, I didn't," she admitted. "I'm really struggling with all that, even telling you. It's just … we've been fighting for so long for a viable pregnancy, and I know it sounds stupid, but I didn't want to jinx it."

"That's not stupid," Chelsea declared warmly. "I want nothing more than for you to have a happy, healthy baby, and I especially don't want you getting stressed out because of this crap going on right now."

"When you find a way to stop the stress," Julie said, "you tell me. We'll bottle it, and we'll all make millions."

"Isn't that the truth?" she muttered.

Once everything that needed to go into the oven at the moment was baking, Chelsea turned her attention to cleaning up the kitchen. By the time they were done with that, she looked around at Julie again. "I feel as if we could do more."

"There is more," Julie replied. "Let's do the prep for dinner."

"Do you think we'll have everybody here by then?"

Julie hesitated. "I have no clue. I don't even know what to think about that question."

"I guess, in that case, let's just plan for everybody to eat dinner here. If you have leftovers, that's a good thing. More for later."

Julie laughed. "Around here, leftovers tend to get incorporated into the next meal, or else it's what I eat."

"Hey, no big deal. I'm always up for leftovers myself," Chelsea said. "I have no problem with that."

"Good." Julie nodded. "If all of them leave and leave unhappy, we could be living on leftovers for a while."

"You're really worried about the business, aren't you?"

"I don't know what I'm worried about," Julie admitted, scrunching up her nose. "It's a whole lot of everything. I can't really pinpoint it, but I'm really not enjoying this season," she muttered. "I wasn't feeling great before these guys arrived either, and I think that's just because I've been so nervous about the baby, but now it definitely has that *off* sense, and I really just want to go home."

"Then maybe that's what you should do. Maybe Rick

can hire a cook to come up here, and you can stay home for a while and rest."

"That sounds appealing, but I really want to be with him," she shared, with a smile.

"I know you want to stay with Rick, yet you have to do what's right for the baby."

She nodded. "I know. I've been thinking about it."

"Is there any reason to suspect that you might need to be home and resting with the baby?" Chelsea asked cautiously. Her sister-in-law hadn't ever been very forthcoming about her other miscarriages.

Now Julie just looked at her and shook her head. "Not that I'm aware of. ... As far as I know, everything is fine, but I haven't had a scan yet."

"Maybe that would be something to ask about when you get back."

"Definitely, but, in the meantime, I have to deal with what's on my plate, and that appears to be this." She gestured to the other room, where the men talked in undertones.

"Right," Chelsea agreed. "In that case, we'll deal with this and do a good job, and then you can go home and take care of Baby. That sounds like a perfect project to carry on with."

Julie laughed. "It's hardly a project. This is a lifetime thing."

"It *is* a lifetime thing, and I don't know two people who deserve it more."

Julie hugged her, sighing. "Thank you for that. I've been so anxious to get pregnant, and now that I am? ... I'm so petrified that I'll be a shitty mother."

"Oh my, no way." Chelsea stared at her, "I don't know

where that's coming from, but you can stop thinking that. You'll be a great mother. Remember that."

"Yeah, not so easy to do," Julie noted, with a grin. "I know it's just nerves, but *just nerves* can still be pretty upsetting."

"Oh, absolutely, and, by the way, there isn't any such thing as *just nerves*. It's *plain old nerves*, so call it what it is and move on."

At that, her sister-in-law burst into laughter. "Sometimes things seem very simple. And sometimes it's not so simple."

"But I do get it in this case," Chelsea explained. "I know I don't have any kids of my own, but I can see that this is something the two of you really want, and one day I would like to have kids myself." She grinned. "So, we'll get through whatever needs to be gotten through here and then get you both home, and you can have a happy, healthy pregnancy."

Just then the oven buzzer rang. Julie walked over and started pulling out cookie sheets.

"Do we need to call the men for breakfast?" Chelsea asked her.

"I have no idea. Maybe that's a question you could go ask Rick."

"I'll do that." Chelsea walked out of the kitchen to talk to Rick, finding all the men gathered there in the front room. Their bags were packed up, and they were ready to leave. She winced, not knowing how this would work out for anybody because Rick needed the business.

As she stood here listening, it was obvious their guests were looking for some of their money back, but Rick wasn't interested in that at all.

"I don't give a shit what you say. You brought a shit ton of trouble with you, and it's raining down on my world too.

With one of your buddies getting shot, bringing the cops up here"—Rick shook his head—"there's no refund for any of your time, and you've already used up three-quarters of your stay here anyway."

"But some of it's left," one of them noted.

"And I'll be dealing with the cops for the rest of that time," Rick muttered. "So, no matter what you say and how it looks to you, there was no indication that you might not stay the whole time when you booked the lodge. So, no, there's no refund. If you're choosing to leave a day or two early, that one's on you."

The men just glared at him. It's not as if they should have expected to catch a break on the pricing. That wasn't how things worked when a murder happened.

As Julie joined them, she announced, "Breakfast is ready."

The men turned, looked at her, then at each other and shrugged. "If that's the case, we might as well eat. We've paid for it."

"Yes, you absolutely have," Rick agreed. He looked over at Walton and the detective, as both left the home office, and walked toward the kitchen. "The men are looking to leave early," Rick told them both.

The detective came down quickly with his veto. "They're not leaving until I get their statements."

At that, the three of them glared at him, and one of them stated, "We had nothing to do with our friend's death."

"Maybe so, but I only have your word on that, and considering that this is now connected to another murder—of *another* one of your friends—I'm really not comfortable seeing you just ride off into the sunset as if it's nothing. This is a murder, and it needs to be sorted out. One way or another, we need to get to the bottom of it."

"We didn't have anything to do with it," Hawk stated. "I'm sure somebody else must have been in the woods. Who knows, maybe Rick here was out shooting."

"An autopsy would let us know what kind of gun was used to kill your friend," the detective noted, "so you just keep that in mind."

The men looked at each other and shrugged, then Hawk shared, "None of our guns were fired. You can ask him for that information."

Rick looked at the three men, then faced the detective. "The guns that these guys got from me weren't fired at all. But those weren't the only guns these guys had that I know about on this trip. My understanding is that you all came up with your own weapons."

"He's right," the detective chimed in. "Just because you were out target shooting and using some of Rick's guns doesn't mean you didn't come with your own."

Walton nodded. "I know damn well that you have your own guns, so maybe, before you leave, the detective needs to have a close look at those too."

The two detectives now studied the three men. "Did you have your own weapons on you when you were out in the woods earlier with Chad?"

Dead silence came, and the lead detective spoke up. "In that case, we'll put you in cuffs, and we will go through your gear to find out exactly what you brought up here. Let's not in any way diminish the fact that this is a murder investigation, and all three of you were there at the time."

"You think we were the only ones up there? What about Walton?" Hawk snapped. "Let's not forget he was there too."

"Oh, I already heard his story," the detective stated, his tone hard, "but now I need to hear each of yours, and not one of you is leaving until I know everything there is to know."

WALTON KEPT AN eye on the men and their bags, as everybody was taken into Rick's office, one by one, for questioning. Walton hadn't been deputized in any way, but he also knew that these men couldn't be trusted, and, between the two of them, Walton and Rick kept an eye on everyone. It was important to ensure that nothing else happened.

Walton also kept his cell phone camera focused on the luggage. When the men were done being questioned, the two detectives came out and quickly went through their gear, and, in total, the cops found four weapons. They shared a look and turned to the men and asked, "Presumably you have licenses for these?"

All three of them nodded. "Yes, we do," Hawk replied.

"That's good, but we'll hold them for forensics, so we can match them against the bullets recovered in autopsy."

The men just glared at each other, as if somehow this was the other's fault. A definite splintering among the remaining *friends* had begun, and Walton liked to see that. It was a good way to divide and conquer. He also wasn't sure that somebody hadn't ditched another weapon near the murder scene.

As he looked at the trio, he suspected that could be a possibility. He looked over at Rick. "Are you okay with this lot?"

"Sure, why?"

He hesitated and then said, "I want to take a walk."

"Yeah, and why is that?" one of the detectives asked, overhearing them.

"Because it occurred to me, now that you have all these weapons, it's quite possible that the shooter ditched the one that shot Chad." The *friends* shuffled angrily at him, and he shrugged. "I'm not saying who might have done it or who didn't. I'm just saying it's a real possibility."

"It is a possibility, but we did do a search in the dark while we were out there," the lead detective pointed out.

"I know, but I want to take the dog and go over that area again." With that, the detectives eyed the War Dog with interest. Walton nodded at them and added, "I would appreciate it if one of you would come with me. Otherwise somebody is bound to make a comment about how I probably threw the weapon in the woods in the first place."

"If you find something, then we'll *know* that you threw the weapon into the woods in the first place," Hawk declared, his tone harsher than needed. "This has just been a big game to you, when you came up here, ready to kill Chad for that dog in the first place."

Walton frowned at him. "Except for the fact that I'm unarmed and that I already got the dog off Chad, remember?"

"Yeah, and, as soon as he produced documentation proving that the dog was his, you would have had to give it back." Hawk snapped, red in the face.

"Considering that he had no such documentation, that wasn't likely, was it? But you bring up an interesting motive. My killing Chad for a dog I already had is an interesting thought."

Hawk shrugged. "I'm just saying, if they searched and didn't find anything at the crime scene …"

"Sure, but they didn't have the War Dog with them," Walton stated, with a lazy smile in their direction. "Believe me when I say that he can sniff out that shit. It depends on what the dog's been trained for, of course, and I've been asking my bosses to track down his training records so we could do just that."

"*Great*," Hawk muttered, "so now you can go plant evidence to make it look like somebody else shot Chad. Yet the whole time it was you."

"Not quite," Rick argued. "He and I reached Chad's body at the same time, but coming from opposite directions. We found all of you already gathered around the body."

"Now, you three, on the other hand," Walton added, "one of you killed Rudy, one of your own, and just decided to take out a second one." Then he held up the USB key. "Plus, we found this on your dead friend's body." They froze as they stared at it. "So, just what kind of friend was Chad?"

They looked at each other uneasily, and finally Hawk admitted, "He was a piece of shit, that's what he was."

"Hey, hey, hey, don't go there now," Darren muttered.

"Why not?" Hawk asked. "Chad blackmailed me into coming on this godforsaken hunting trip with him and look how that's turned out."

"I know," Darren replied, "but we can't really blame the guy. He was trying to figure out who the hell killed Rudy."

"Sure, and how did you guys end up coming?" Walton asked the others.

"I had to come because he would tell my girlfriend about something in my past that I didn't want her to know about," George shared ruefully.

"Oh, shit." The lead detective was now looking at them with interest. "Did Chad really blackmail you?"

"Yeah, and if it's on that goddamn key, … I want it," George declared, glaring at Walton.

"It'll be held in evidence, and I'll leave it with the detectives for now," Walton shared, as he handed it over. "We found it in Chad's boots."

"Oh yeah? And what if you planted that too?" Hawk snapped again.

"I have a witness in Rick, who also took a timestamped video. I'm sure the authorities can forensically tell whose evidence it was," Walton noted, staring at him. "We don't even know what's on the USB, and we don't really give a shit. The last thing we want is anything to do with you guys and your dirty little secrets, but it might have been enough info to kill one if not two people," he explained to the group of suspects. "So the USB and the blackmail now becomes something that the authorities will take a look at."

The lead detective looked over at each of the men, one at a time. "If somebody's got something to say, this would be a really good time to say it."

"I already said it," Hawk grumbled. "Chad was a piece of shit, and he blackmailed me into coming here."

"Are you interested in telling us why?" the detective asked, holding the USB in his hand, looking at it.

"It's stupid. It's nothing even big, but I know it would piss off my wife, and, for the first time, I found somebody I care about," he shared.

"So, what's the big secret all about?" the lead detective asked.

Hawk sighed. "I have a child. … It's something I haven't acknowledged. It's also a child my wife knows because the mother of the child is my wife's best friend."

"Holy shit, you banged her best friend?" the second detective asked.

"I did, but it was a long time ago," Hawk snapped. "I didn't even know they were friends at the time. This was before I even met my wife, before we got married."

"Does the best friend know her kid is yours? Does the kid know you're his father?"

"No," he snapped, "nobody knows anything, but I do. The kid's a spitting image of my dad, and the timing is kind of right on for this one. Chad, the asshole that he was, obviously thought so too because he was using it to blackmail me."

"Dude, that sucks," muttered the ever-quiet George. "I had no idea."

"No, and, of course, now you'll go blab it."

"No, I won't," George declared. "I've got my own problems." He hesitated, looked at the key, and shrugged. "Chad was blackmailing me too."

"What?" Darren turned and looked at him in shock.

"Yeah, he also blackmailed me to come on this goddamn trip of his."

"Interesting," Walton muttered, as he looked from one guest to the other. "Darren, what about you? Is that the same tactic Chad used on you?"

Darren bristled. After looking from one face to the other, his shoulders sagged, and he finally nodded. "Yeah, you could say that. The guys don't know about me, and they'll want nothing to do with me afterward, but I'm gay. I'm not out. Well, I guess I am now, ... but I'm so goddamn tired of this rigamarole."

"Dude, what the fuck are you saying? ... We all knew

anyway," Hawk declared, staring at him.

Darren stared back, saying, "What?"

"Yeah, it's pretty-damn obvious, and I didn't give a shit." Hawk turned to George.

George shrugged. "I knew too. Nothing much to overthink there. It's not as if that's a big deal."

"You may not think so, but my parents don't know, and Chad was going to tell them." Darren frowned at them and asked, confusion on his face, "You guys really don't care?"

"No, of course we don't give a shit. You're not trying to come on to us, so what do we care?" Hawk asked, with half a laugh. "But I can see how that would be something Chad would use as a weapon because he was all about utilizing whatever he could to turn the screw on us a little more."

"Yeah, he sure as hell was," Darren muttered. "And you know that, if my parents find out, I'm completely ruined. It would really be a hot mess."

"Yeah, I'm sorry, man. Your dad's really old-school."

"So is my mother, so pretty much everything in my world would go to pieces."

"But I thought you were getting married to Elena?" George asked.

"No, I've got a boyfriend, but Elena is a good friend to me. She's cool, and she just covers for me."

"And that's too bad too," George noted. "You should be able to live your life as you want to."

"I agree, but it seemed everybody wanted me to keep it hidden, you know, *to keep the family disgrace under the covers, so to speak.*"

"Literally," Hawk said, with a big grin.

Darren laughed. "I know. I know. I was even married for ten years, so who knew? But, … he makes me happy."

"Dude," George shared, "if he makes you happy, you've got to go for it. That's more than any of us has had in these last several years. Don't let anybody steal your joy from you."

Darren looked over at his friends, grateful and clearly relieved. "Thank you for that."

The lead detective cleared his throat. "Now all of this is fine and dandy, but what else will we find on that USB key?" The detective gazed from one to the other. "Did you guys know anything about Rudy? Did he have a secret too?"

"Shit, I don't know." Hawk shrugged, looking over at his buddies. "Did any of you guys ever hear of anything?"

They both frowned. George replied, "I don't think so, but that would mean that you're thinking—no, that wouldn't make sense. It's not as if Chad would have killed Rudy—unless it was …" He looked from one to the other. "Unless it was self-defense because of something that Rudy did to Chad. Maybe Rudy had enough of Chad and attacked him. Maybe he … lost it on Chad. I could see that happening."

"In which case then it would have been self-defense, so nobody should have been charged," the second detective noted.

"Nobody *should* be charged," George clarified.

"And that's possible," the detective replied grumpily, "but we're not there yet."

"No, of course you're not there yet," George muttered, with a groan. "Sometimes this shit just never *gets there* either."

The lead detective sighed. "Remember that we're not directly involved in Rudy's murder investigation, other than file sharing because you same guys are involved with both murders now. We will do our best with our investigation into Chad's murder, but, if you guys keep lying and withholding information," the lead detective pointed out, "it's pretty hard to get the full story so we can do a proper investigation."

"You've got my info from me now," Hawk noted. "I don't have anything else to tell you, and I really just want to go home."

"Why don't you guys go eat, while we finish going through all your stuff and getting it all logged in," the lead detective suggested. "Then you'll be free to go, but expect us to contact you afterward as needed."

"*Great*," Hawk muttered.

By the time everybody had eaten something and was loaded up and ready to leave, Hawk turned to Walton and shared, "Chad would have beaten up that old guy for the dog, you know?"

"I do know," Walton confirmed, "and that's yet another case the authorities will have to look into."

"You might want to tell these guys that."

"Already did," Walton noted.

The detectives turned to him and asked, "What was that?"

Walton repeated what he'd shared with the lead guy earlier.

"By the way," the lead detective added, "I was notified earlier that the old guy just died."

Hawk, the color in his face now completely drained, muttered, "Jesus. Seriously?"

"Yeah, he died from complications of the head injury."

"Well, crap." Hawk stared over at the vehicle containing Chad's body. "All of that over a dog. Jesus, Chad." And, with that, he walked toward their own vehicle. Looking back, he called out, "Come on, you guys. Let's get the hell out of here. As holidays go, this one sucks big-time."

"Yeah, I just want to get home to my gal," George said, with a sigh. "She'll never believe this shit."

Chelsea slipped her hand into Walton's. He smiled at her and gently squeezed her hand, while tugging her a little closer. They watched as the three men got into their two vehicles and drove away. Then he turned and looked at the detectives. "I still want to have a look in the woods."

"We'll all come with you," Detective Hogan replied. "Then we need to get going too, before the body gets ripe."

"Good idea," Walton said, "but I do want to see if we can utilize the dog a little more." With that, he headed toward the woods, Brutus beside him. Brutus moved easily, the hitch in his gait not slowing him down. Rick was following along, as was Detective McKenna. Brutus was taking the lead.

"What will you do with the injured War Dog?" Detective Hogan asked.

"Not sure yet," Walton replied. "He got that injury while saving some friends of mine. It took me a bit to find out the full story, but you can bet that, as far as I'm concerned, he gets to live the rest of his life in the best way possible."

"How did you get the story on Brutus?" Chelsea asked.

"Badger texted it to me this morning," he shared, with a smile. "He is also the one who told me how the old man had passed away from his injuries too, which really pisses me off." He sighed. "He was another war vet, and he didn't deserve that shit."

"It sounds as if Chad was a piece of shit all the way around," she muttered. "Does all that mean you get to keep

Brutus?"

"Badger and Kat are looking into it, and, if I can make it happen, I will," he declared. "Brutus needs somebody to be his champion for a change."

"And you'll keep his current name?" she asked, as she walked at his side.

"Not if I can help it. It doesn't fit him at all."

"No, it really doesn't," Detective Hogan agreed, as the five of them followed Brutus to where the body had been.

When they reached the crime scene area, McKenna looked back at Rick and asked, "Do you have it?"

Rick pulled out a small handgun and a bullet.

"What's that for?" Chelsea asked.

"It's just for GSR," Walton replied. "Gunshot residue."

McKenna asked Rick to fire it off to the side, which he did, and then passed over the handgun for the War Dog to sniff. Walton then made the hand gesture for Brutus to go ahead and to find more.

"Now what'll stop him from chasing the bullet?" McKenna asked.

"He might find a bullet too or even a casing," Walton noted, "but there's a good chance Brutus will find more than that."

"Can he really smell GSR after all this time?" McKenna asked.

"Absolutely," Walton declared. "What these dogs can do is amazing."

Barely ten minutes had gone by when they heard a bark, and everybody raced toward Brutus. Sure enough, as Walton pulled back the tall brush, there was a handgun, mostly buried under leaves and debris. He looked over at the detectives. "Does that answer your question?"

Swearing, they pulled out gloves, picked it up, and nodded. "Yep, that's a really good start." McKenna smiled at the dog. "You know, with training like the two of you have, the police force could use some help at times, if you're staying in the area."

"Alaska is home for me, although not this general area," Walton replied, "so it's possible. I know that Brutus likes to work, and most War Dogs have this training."

"Even at the airport, we're always looking for animals that are well-trained."

"That could be interesting too. Maybe you want to be a sniffer dog, *huh*, buddy? Would you like that?"

Brutus woofed several times and pranced around, happy with the attention.

McKenna noted, "He seems to have a good temperament."

"He does. Yet he couldn't run down and track people full-time because of his leg, but he's absolutely still in the game."

"Obviously."

They all watched as the detectives removed the bullet that Rick had shot into the ground, and then, with that safely stored away too, they looked over at Walton and asked, "What do you think the deal is here?"

"If three bullets were in Chad, I would have said all three were the killers." Walton shrugged. "With just two bullets, I'll say two people. The only question is whether they both fired or not."

"What do you mean?"

"I heard the two shots," he recalled, "and it was really rapid fire."

At that, Rick nodded. "That's right. There wasn't really

any time for the gun to be passed to someone else, unless both hands were over it at the same time."

"And that's possible," McKenna noted.

"You heard what the guys said," Walton pointed out. "Chad brought a lot of blackmail and a lot of misery to their lives, so it could likely be any one of them. It is also likely that two of them worked in concert, but we don't know enough. At least not yet."

"When you say, *not yet*, what do you mean?"

Walton shrugged. "I suspect we're just at the tip of finding out what's really going on right now. It could very well … Look. I really don't want to put it out there, but I'm not entirely sure they'll all get home safely."

At that, the detectives stared at each other, then back at him. Detective McKenna frowned. "I sure as hell hope you're wrong."

"Me too, but I've got a pretty-ugly feeling about those guys."

"In that case let's get moving," Detective Hogan said. "We'll come up behind them wherever they are."

"That's another reason I wanted you to leave after them. They're in two vehicles, though I didn't get a chance to see who's in which rig, but that's something we'll have to take a look at."

"Are you staying here?" McKenna asked Walton.

Hesitating, he looked over at Chelsea, then shook his head. "I need to get back."

Chelsea nodded. "In that case, I'll go pack my things," and she quickly disappeared.

Walton looked at the detectives and added, "Honestly, this all still feels incredibly wrong."

Picking up on his unease, both detectives nodded.

"That's fine. We're heading back ourselves right now," Hogan stated.

Quickly bagging the evidence, they walked back to the lodge, and the two cops got into their own vehicles and disappeared.

Rick looked over at Walton. "You don't have to leave, you know?"

"I don't have to, but it feels very much like I should."

"Not because of a problem here, I hope."

"No, not at all," Walton countered, with a smile. "You guys need to enjoy a few days with no drama. Julie needs to have a chance to calm down and relax. Those men were pretty rough on her."

"They were," Rick agreed, "and we do have more people coming in a couple days. So we'll stock up and get everything sorted out and reset for that."

"And you need to spend some time thinking about what you're doing because I don't think Julie's particularly impressed with the idea of continuing this."

Rick's eyebrows popped up. "Seriously?"

"Yeah, but I'm pretty sure it's due to the pregnancy. So, if you've got a cook you can hire, and maybe your ranch hand can take over in your stead, that would help. I'm just saying, you might need to rethink your options."

"Well, shit," Rick muttered. "This was what we both always wanted."

"It's what you always wanted *preconception*. Now Julie wants that child more than the lodge."

Rick looked over at him and nodded in understanding. "Got it," he said, with a smile. "Hopefully she will enjoy it again, after the baby is here."

"She probably will, but right now she'll be in nesting

mode, and that may be fine here, or it might very well be something that she wants to change. So maybe just talk to her about it. Plus, have a deeper look into your guests before allowing them here."

He laughed. "I've already been talking to her about all that, but maybe she's just been waiting for the right time to talk to me about staying at home for a while."

"In that case, you should be happy we're leaving. It'll give you a few days to get your heads on straight."

"Only if you come back and bring my sister, so she can enjoy some quality time here. I get why this visit happened, but she won't ever come back now, unless I force her."

"We'll come back," Walton confirmed. "If for nothing else but to enjoy the countryside because it truly is beautiful here."

When he got back to the lodge, Chelsea had brought down his stuff too and was waiting for him. When he looked at her with one eyebrow raised, she shrugged.

"Believe me that I get it. It's time to go." She walked over, gave her brother a big hug and a kiss and warned him to look after Julie. Then she did the same to her sister-in-law, warning her to look after her brother. With everybody laughing, Walton and Chelsea got into his vehicle, and minutes later were racing down the road.

CHAPTER 11

"**A**RE YOU OKAY?" Chelsea asked, after they'd been driving for a few minutes. When he frowned over at her, she shrugged. "You seem pretty intense."

"Yeah, I don't know why really," he said, "but something just doesn't feel right."

"No, I definitely get that too," she murmured. "I don't know that it has anything to do with us though."

"No, probably not," he agreed, with a smile in her direction. "But I don't want Detectives Hogan and McKenna to get caught up in something they aren't expecting either."

She stared at him, confused for a moment. "Are you expecting us to get caught up in something too?"

"I hope not," he muttered. "I just don't know what is bothering me about this whole deal."

"Did you see everybody standing around Chad's body right after the two shots were fired?"

Walton nodded. "I saw them all there. By the time I arrived at Chad's body, all three men were there."

"And you still think that two of them had something to do with shooting Chad?"

He shrugged. "I could easily be wrong, and that's the problem. I just don't know what's going on, but something is seriously wrong with this whole picture."

"I wish they would speak up about their dead friend

Rudy too. What the hell was that all about?"

"Wouldn't that be nice to have honesty from suspects," Walton quipped, with a nod. "I don't know that these guys are capable of telling the truth."

"Oh my God," she whispered. "You think they all lied?"

"I don't know if they lied or not, but I'm definitely suspicious of anything that comes out of their mouths. I have an itch here that I can't scratch."

"Wow, okay then," she muttered. "That's understandable. I hope that you're wrong though, and that we get home without any trouble."

"Me too."

They drove down the highway for several more minutes. Walton got a text. Walton glanced at the screen, his cell phone propped up on the dashboard, but immediately returned his gaze to the roadway. He didn't say anything, so Chelsea left it alone.

Chelsea asked him, "They should be quite a distance ahead of us, right?"

"They should be," he agreed, with a nod, "but that doesn't mean they are."

"Okay then," she noted. As they kept on going, she felt the uneasiness rising up in her gut. "I don't know what the hell's going on," she muttered, "but you're making me nervous." When he turned to her, she shrugged. "Now I've got your heebie-jeebies."

He chuckled. "*Heebie-jeebies.* I like that term."

She groaned. "You might like it, but I don't. It just makes me realize how wrong some of this is."

"*All* of it is," he stated, "and that's the trouble. Once you start down that pathway of lies and deceit, nobody knows who the hell's telling the truth."

"Maybe," she said, "and maybe it's something completely different."

"We won't know if one of them doesn't speak up. And they're bound and determined not to. They've already lost two of their friends, and, although they might have their suspicions, they're most likely to only voice those suspicions privately."

"So," she began, "if they do it to the wrong person …" He looked over at her, and she nodded. "Right, if they do it to the wrong person, they'll likely end up dead."

He nodded. "If somebody's trying to hide one murder—and now a second one—it's possible that they'll do anything they can to avoid getting caught now."

"Crap," she muttered. "How did we get involved in any of this?"

"My fault. I was chasing a War Dog."

"Your fault but not your fault," she clarified, glancing over at him. "It's not as if you had anything to do with their killing each other. Why couldn't they have just done it all on their own, without involving anybody else?"

"Wouldn't that have been nice? On the other hand," he noted, with a smile, "we got to spend some quality time together."

She brightened, then looked over at him. "I want to spend more time with you," she admitted.

"That would make me really happy," he shared. "I was trying to get into better shape, so I could come back and not be a broken model. At least not as broken."

"I never saw you as broken," she declared. "I saw you as this determined, stalwart, but incredibly strong individual, who was doing everything he could to pull himself back out of a horrific injury." He looked at her, and she smiled. "I don't think we ever see ourselves as other people do, and I think sometimes we need to stop, take stock, and realize that it's not all bad. In your case, you fought so hard to get back on your feet, to get full movement, and then you were gone."

"It wasn't that I was gone," he clarified, a bit abashed.

"You *were* gone," she declared.

He winced, his gaze flicking her way before going back to the road again. "Maybe, and, for that, I'm sorry."

"No apologies necessary," she said, "at least now I know why." Then she laughed. "Honestly, I could probably help you get up to the next level, versus you trying to do it on your own."

"I know. You're right. I was just …" He winced. "I'll put that down to pride."

"Yeah, I will too," she added, with a groan. "I'm telling you that male pride is nothing to mess with. It can be brutal and causes a lot of bad decisions."

He laughed. "Honest to God, it's one of the worst things ever. We're not that fragile, until something goes wrong, and then we are as fragile as anyone."

As they came around a corner, a good twenty minutes into the trip, she asked, "Do you think they're up ahead?" Walton remained silent. She looked over at him and asked again, "Do you?"

He looked at her and nodded. "Yeah, I think they're up ahead."

"You're really expecting something bad, aren't you?"

"I'm hoping not."

"And yet you're speeding like crazy."

He took his foot off the accelerator and sighed. She watched his shoulders relaxing somewhat. "So, you're really expecting something bad. That's good to know. *Not.*"

"Now you're bracing for it," he pointed out, "and that's not what I wanted."

"Of course not," she stated in a hard tone. "I don't want it either, but we also know that it'll likely turn up right here in front of us."

"I'm afraid it is," he declared and hit the brakes.

She saw the two police vehicles up ahead. "Oh, crap."

THEY PULLED UP behind the closest cop car, as Walton shut down the engine to his truck and got out. No sign of anybody was here. He called down the nearby ravine, and one of the detectives answered him. Walton had no idea if it was McKenna or Hogan, but it was definitely one of them.

"Stay up there," he yelled at Walton.

Walton waited, as one of them climbed up from the ravine and stepped onto the highway. It was Detective McKenna. "What the hell happened?" Walton asked him.

"One of the vehicles went off the road and over the edge."

"Shit," he said, looking at McKenna.

"We don't know that it's foul play though. Remember that."

"No, of course not. Is somebody dead?"

"Yes, two dead bodies are down there."

"Two?" Walton asked, staring at him.

"Yes, the vehicle went over at full speed," he added.

"What about the other vehicle?"

"It was in the lead, so no need for it to stop. He wouldn't have seen the accident."

"Unless he saw it in the rearview mirror. Unless he cut

the brakes and wanted it to happen."

"Maybe," Detective McKenna replied, as Detective Hogan now joined them. "We'll have to catch up with the third guy down the road, but, right now, we've got to call this in and get some help up here."

Walton looked from Detective Hogan to Detective McKenna. "Are you guys heading back down there?"

"That was the plan," McKenna said, staring down the ravine.

"I will head down now and see what I can do," Hogan added, as he started down.

Walton asked, "Are you sure you see no evidence of foul play?"

Detective McKenna shrugged. "Not for me to say, but it looks as if they went straight off the road. Could have had an argument, could have been an accident," he suggested. "It's a hell of a corner."

Walton had to agree because it *was* a hell of a corner. Chelsea had tears in her eyes as she came out of the vehicle with Brutus, who stood on the road and whined.

"I know, buddy," Walton told the War Dog, "but nothing good is down there for us." He looked at Detective McKenna. "I really would appreciate it if you would treat this like a crime scene."

Detective McKenna stiffened and stated, "We do know how to do our jobs."

"I know you do," Walton replied, raising his hands. "I did warn both of you earlier that something like this could likely happen."

The detective studied him for a long moment and then nodded. "We're taking every possible precaution. You guys don't need to be here. It's better if you carry on, and we'll get this taken care of. We'll be in touch."

Walton wasn't sure what that meant about *being in touch*, but he nodded because it was obvious the detectives wanted them out of the way.

As they stepped back over toward his vehicle, another vehicle barreled around the corner from the other direction. It stopped when it saw them. Darren got out and raced toward Walton. "What the hell happened?" he cried out, visibly shaken.

The detective grabbed him by the shoulders and snapped, "Calm down."

"Are they okay? Where's the vehicle? They were behind me, and then they weren't. I slowed down, but they weren't behind me. I got worried and came back. What the hell's going on?"

The detective replied, "They drove off the road."

Darren crumpled to his knees, just staring at the detective, then jumped up. "Let's go get them. I'll help. Where are they?" he asked frantically, moving to the cliff's edge.

"No," Detective McKenna said, grabbing him and pulling him back. "You can't go down there."

Walton knew exactly why he couldn't go down there, but it was obvious that Darren didn't have a clue.

"Why not? My friends are down there."

"I know." Detective McKenna hesitated and then relented. "It doesn't appear that anyone survived the accident."

Darren stared at him in shock, then started to cry in big, ugly, uncontrollable sobs. "No, no, no, no. We just came up here for a holiday. We came up here for a long weekend, for a few days together," he mumbled to himself. "This can't be happening."

"I'm very sorry," McKenna said, "but I can tell you that

nobody survived down there. We have local police and search and rescue coming."

"Search and rescue?" he asked.

"Yes, search-and-rescue. The vehicle needs to be dealt with, and your friends need to be brought up."

Darren just stared at him, still not comprehending in full yet. But, when he dropped to the ground, he seemed to understand.

Chelsea walked over and sat down beside him, a hand on his shoulder. "Take it easy, Darren. I know this is pretty rough news."

He shook his head, his gaze unfocused. "It just can't be," he said. "I mean, we were going into town to have a few beers. How can everybody be gone?"

Something the detective said had piqued Walton's interest. Walking over to him, he asked in a low tone, "Are there two bodies?"

He nodded. "We definitely found two bodies, and, as you saw, my partner's down there right now."

Walton asked, "Would you mind if I go down there with Brutus?"

"What good would that do?" he asked.

He hesitated, then spoke. "I don't know. I'm going by instincts here."

Detective McKenna considered his request and then shrugged. "It's on you, be my guest, but don't contaminate the crime scene."

"I hear you." Walton walked over to the edge of the road, looked back at Chelsea, and added, "I'll be back in a few minutes." Her eyebrows shot up as he smiled. "It'll be fine." Then he stepped over the edge with Brutus.

"No, no, no," she cried out.

He heard her in the background but knew that the detective would stop her. He made his way down to the bottom of the hill where the wreckage was. The vehicle had flipped multiple times, and not a whole lot was left inside. He walked over to where Detective Hogan was taking photos. "Hey," Walton hailed him. "You found both bodies?"

The detective frowned at him and then nodded. "They're both here."

"It's not that I don't believe you, but I wanted to take a look myself."

"Okay, do you want to explain that?"

"No, I don't really understand myself. I guess I want to see the victims, since I met them all back at the lodge."

Hogan pointed to where the first body was.

Walton took a closer look. Walton nodded. "That's definitely Hawk."

"Yeah, it sure is, or at least what's left of him," Detective Hogan said, irony in his tone, "if that's what you came down here for."

As they circled the crash site, Walton asked, "Where's the other body?"

"He was flipped over there," Hogan pointed out.

And, with that, Walton headed to where the body had done a complete flip, and, indeed, the remains of a broken man were on the ground. Walton studied the body for a long moment and wondered if he could possibly be wrong.

Detective Hogan came over. "This is George."

Walton studied the body and shook his head. "I am not so sure about that."

"What do you mean?"

"I am not so sure that it is."

"Who else would it be?"

"It'll be the missing friend that they've not been forth-coming about. They were certainly hiding something, or in this case, … someone."

"Whoa, whoa, whoa. You're telling me this is another friend who is dead? Not George?"

"Yeah, I'm pretty-damn sure yet another *friend* is dead," Walton shared, "and it appears to me that this is him. *Not* George."

"No, no, that can't be," Hogan frowned. "Or is it really possible?"

"One of the things I recently found out, when my boss did a deeper dive into these friends, is that George had a brother, a twin brother." When Hogan glared at him, Walton added, "My boss just told me. I can show you the timestamped text that I got while driving here this morning."

"So, you think this is him, the twin?"

"I think it's quite possibly him. The body is broken, as in quite badly broken. DNA with an identical twin will give us the same results, twice, from what I understand."

"Well, shit," Hogan muttered. "What makes you think this isn't George?"

"I noticed a scar on George's face, just behind the hairline, but there is no hairline left on this body," he noted.

"So, what you're telling me is that the one bit of evidence that might direct us to tell the difference between two identical twins is not here anymore?"

"Exactly."

Hogan swore. "That's a hell of a thing, and I hear you. Now, just go on up, take care of your girlfriend and the War Dog, and let us do our job."

Knowing it would be useless to say anything else, Walton nodded and slowly climbed up the hill. Finding the other detective on the phone at his car and Chelsea still sitting beside Darren, Walton walked over and crouched down in front of them. "What happened to George's brother?" he asked Darren.

He looked up at him, blinked, and shrugged. "I don't know really. They had a falling out, but some peacemaking was in progress. Then another falling out occurred and more peacemaking. I don't know what the hell happened after that."

"George had a brother?" Chelsea asked.

Walton nodded. "Yeah, he did, but not anymore." And on that cryptic note, he stood up and announced, "We need to leave."

"What about Darren here?" she asked.

"I'm staying until my friends are taken away," Darren replied, as he stared down at the ravine. "I don't have a clue what the hell's going on, but my friends are all gone. Every last one of them," he whispered.

Not knowing what else to say to him, Walton urged Chelsea to get up. "Ready to go home?"

She frowned at him, pointing back to Darren.

Walton nodded. "Darren, do you want us to give you a lift home?"

He stared at them. "No, I've got to return the rental."

"I'm sure the cops could arrange that," Walton suggested.

"No, no," he replied. "I'll be fine, honestly. I just need to see my friends."

"Good enough." Walton helped Chelsea to her feet. "Come on. Time to go home."

They got into his truck, and very slowly he pulled out

onto the road. This time he drove much slower.

"You were half expecting that, weren't you?" she asked.

"I don't know if I was expecting *that*," he clarified. "I was expecting something, but what I got was a whole lot more than anticipated."

"That makes absolutely no sense to me," she replied. "I wish you wouldn't speak in riddles."

"I'm sorry." He gave her a smile. "That's not what I was trying to do. I still haven't figured out what I just found."

"Ah, well, I guess it's okay. You'll piece it together soon enough."

He chuckled. "Thank you."

She smiled. "It's just very disturbing to see that."

He immediately felt bad. "You're right. I should have thought of that."

She gave a wave of her hand. "It is not your fault. Stop trying to make everything your fault."

"I'm not trying to make anything my fault," he protested.

"No, but you're not exactly letting go of stuff," she pointed out, with a smile. "I feel sorry for Darren and for whatever the hell was going on in their world. I hope the cops get to the bottom of it, but I am not at all blaming you."

"Good." He smiled again. "Let's go home and finally get some sleep."

"Didn't you get any sleep last night?" she asked him.

"Nope, I sure didn't. Rick and I took over for the ranch hand, guarding the body. We didn't want anyone to take away or to leave evidence or to in any way alter the crime scene. We were waiting for the police to come, plus checking on you two back at the lodge, so we kept taking turns."

"Jesus. Sitting out there with the dead body? Walking back and forth in the dead of night?"

"I know, and honestly, I should have just brought the body to the lodge, but, for some reason, I thought it would be better out there."

"You did what you thought was right at the time." She shrugged. "No one can blame you for that."

"You'll be surprised at what people can blame me for," he teased, with another smile. "It doesn't really matter though. We got this far, and that's fine. Now I just want to get you home and get you safely back where you belong."

"And where do I belong?" she asked, with a chuckle.

Walton smiled as he looked at her. "With me." When she stared at him in shock, he shrugged. "That sounded a little more possessive than I intended it to be, but I meant it in the best way possible."

"I won't say that we don't know each other because obviously we do, and I won't say that I'm not interested because obviously I am, but that statement definitely came out of left field."

"Yeah, I'm a little out of practice."

"Practice doesn't mean a damn thing to me," she said, "but what is it exactly that you're thinking of here?"

"Just getting to know each other," he replied, "if that's of interest."

"Absolutely it's of interest," she stated, staring at him. "This has been a pretty unsettling couple of days."

"Yeah, it sure has been," he agreed. "For all of us really, but you've handled it beautifully."

"I don't think I've handled anything," she groaned. "It just seems as if everything's gone to shit."

He burst out laughing. "That's not a bad way to look at

it. I like that description myself, though I know it's foolish," he muttered.

"It isn't that far off. We see a dead man near the lodge and then a car accident with two men who we spent the last couple days with, and now they're dead too," she noted, the horror still clear in her tone.

He nodded. "I don't think you should be alone tonight."

She shot him a glance. "Why is that?" she asked.

There was just enough confusion or almost suspicion in her tone that he frowned at her. "I'm not trying to pull one over on you. I just don't think it's a good idea for you to be alone right now."

"I'm not sure I want to be alone," she agreed. "I was just trying to figure out why you even suggested that."

He didn't know how much to tell her. Honestly, he didn't know if he should tell her anything because none of this made any sense. "You're tired and stressed out, and you've been through a lot. How many more reasons do you need? Besides, I like knowing that you're right next door."

"Ah, so what do you want to do? Go to a hotel, so you can sleep on one side of an adjoining room, and I can sleep on the other?" she asked in a teasing tone.

Glad that she wasn't angry at his suggestion, he smiled. "I don't think we have to go that crazy," he murmured, "but your place will seem awfully empty, and I don't want you waking up in the middle of the night over what happened. Things like these can creep up on any of us."

"And that could definitely be the case," she muttered. "But I didn't see Chad's body or those other two. You did. That couldn't have been easy for you either."

"Maybe not easy," he clarified, "but it was something I needed to do."

"I'll never understand that," she muttered. "How is it you needed to do that?"

Again he didn't know how much to tell her, so he just stayed quiet.

"Why don't you spend the night at my place?" she suggested. "We can grab some sleep and talk about it in the morning."

"That sounds good," he replied casually. She glanced over at him with suspicion on her face, and he laughed. "Honest, I'm not making any moves."

"Ha. Good thing. I'm way too tired for moves anyway."

"Exactly. We're both exhausted. It's been a pretty rough few days, and obviously things are still not settled as far as everything else that's going on."

"Right, and I'm not sure it'll ever be settled after what we just saw," she declared. "It's definitely not how I thought this would end." She hesitated and then added, "I can't seem to shake the feeling that you're keeping something from me."

He glanced at her and nodded. "I wouldn't say I'm keeping anything from you. I just haven't sorted through everything that's gone on."

"I would think not," she said. "Everything keeps on happening in front of us."

"If I ever figure out what is bothering me, I will be happy to tell you. In the meantime, it's just guesses and absolutely nothing of any value."

"At least it's over though," she said, "and I don't have to worry about those guys anymore."

"Absolutely," he agreed, with a smile in her direction. "It's not the nicest way to have it be over, but at least it's pretty cut-and-dried."

"I think that's the part that makes me feel bad, the finality of it. It is over, and, no, it's not the nicest thing, but I'm glad that it is that cut-and-dried," she explained. "There was something creepy, yet not creepy about them, but creepy about the way they all acted together. Like the one guy mentioned about them all being under Chad's control, and that was creepy in itself," she muttered.

"I get it."

"I know you do. You would never have anybody under your control. Everybody needs to be in control of themselves. They all should stand on their own two feet. Anybody who wants control over others generally has serious issues."

"Pretty sure we can agree that these guys *all* had some issues."

"Maybe not the same problems, but they definitely had troubles. I still don't understand what the hell they were all doing up there," she muttered.

"They were doing exactly what Chad told them to do. They were making an effort to bond."

"A bonding effort," she repeated, shaking her head. "How is that even a bonding effort when you are forced into it?" She slumped back into the seat and yawned.

He smiled at her and said, "Have a nap. I'll wake you up when we get closer."

She hesitated. "Are you sure you don't need me to stay awake for you?"

"No, I'm fine," he replied, with a wave of his hand. "Go ahead and doze off. It'll be good for you."

"Yeah, you say that now."

"I mean it. Go ahead."

And it wasn't long before he heard her snoring. He should text Badger, but then his phone would be lit up with responses and more questions. Something odd was going on here, and it was a little farfetched for Walton to truly believe it, yet it was hard not to.

When she woke up a little later, they were still on the road. She yawned and asked, "How far?"

"About another forty minutes or so," he guessed.

She frowned at him. "Wow, I really slept, didn't I?"

"You really did," he said in amusement. "You sound surprised."

"I don't normally sleep in vehicles," she muttered. "I don't usually like being a passenger either." When he looked at her in surprise, she shrugged. "It hasn't been an issue with you, so that's another funny thing."

"It just means that you feel safe," he noted. "That's good. So accept it and move on." She burst out laughing again, and he smiled. "See? You think it's good too."

Very quickly they headed into one of the nearby towns, and she suggested that a bathroom break would be good. "Yeah, I got you there," he replied. They pulled into a gas station, and, while he filled up with fuel, she went into the bathroom and then took Brutus to do his business. When she came back out, he added, "I'll go use the facilities, and then I could use a coffee." They met inside the café and ordered coffee to go. "I really do just want to keep on going, but only if you're okay with that."

"I just want this over with," she muttered. "That was all just so creepy."

He smiled and nodded. "No excuses, no reasons needed. Let's just keep moving."

CHAPTER 12

WHEN THEY ARRIVED at Chelsea's house, she was tired, worn out, and yet still amped-up in a way. She sighed, as she looked up at her house and smiled. "It's still lights-out here."

"It absolutely is, and it's fine," he replied. "Let's go in and get you settled. I'm happy to stay the night, or I can go home, whatever you're comfortable with."

"I'm not sending you away now," she declared. "You drove all the way home. The least I can do is feed you."

He smiled. "I sure won't say no to a meal."

"I'm not even sure I have any food," she muttered. "There may be something, but probably not much. So that could be a limiting factor."

He chuckled. "It wouldn't be the worst thing in the world if we ordered something in."

"Julie would be horrified."

"No way, she of all people would understand," he replied.

She looked over at him and nodded. "I'm really glad you met them. They really liked you."

"I don't think they liked anything about me in the first place," he noted, with a big grin, as he unloaded their bags. "I think they were worried that I was a cripple and that you had some savior complex."

She stared at him. "Wow, you got all that from a couple days with my brother?"

"Yeah, I sure did," he declared, with a smile. "But then again, I really liked Rick too. He's just worried about you, and I can understand his point of view."

They walked into the house, and she groaned with joy, spinning around and crying out, making Brutus jump and bark happily at her side. "Is there anything quite like home?"

"Nope." He smiled as he looked at her. "I'm glad you're happy to be back."

"I am definitely happy to be back," she muttered. She walked around to the kitchen and then asked him, "How about some coffee?"

"No thanks, I'm pretty well *coffeed* out."

"Okay, so what about … What do you want to do?"

"I thought you would feed me," he said, with a smile, but then shook his head. "Yeah, I'm not quite ready to eat though."

"Okay, unless you are," she noted.

He shook his head. "I think I'm pretty good. That would be nice later though."

She caught the expression on his face. Out of nowhere, he suddenly stood in front of her. She was about to say something when he snatched her up in his arms and planted a huge, long kiss on her lips.

When he finally lifted his head, she sagged against him and whispered, "Wow. I wasn't expecting that."

"Yes, you were, just maybe not right now."

She smiled and nodded. "You're right, maybe not now."

"Are you okay with the timing?"

"I'm absolutely okay with the timing," she said. "I kept waiting for you to come back for your next appointment, and, when you never booked it, you broke my heart. I put so much time and effort into making sure you were happy and healthy and all that good stuff, but then I never heard from you again." She looked up at him. "You have no idea how crushed I was."

He frowned, then leaned over and kissed her gently on her temple. "I'm sorry. I wasn't trying to hurt you."

"I know," she muttered, "you weren't trying, but we had spent a lot of time together. We were working together a lot, and I thought we had a great rapport. I was hoping you would ask me out, and instead you just ghosted me."

"I never ghosted you," he protested, but then he thought about it and shrugged. "I guess maybe from your perspective I did. But I was just trying to come back bigger, better, stronger, so you didn't feel as if you needed to nursemaid me."

"I never *nursemaided* you," she stated in astonishment. "Needing physical therapy isn't a nursemaid thing. I'm not a nurse. I'm not a doctor. I didn't save your life," she explained and kept on going. "I've simply been helping you reach your highest potential, be the best you can be, and that is a completely different story."

He smiled, then nodded. "I'm glad to hear that."

"I can't believe you disappeared from my world to have *surgeries* and never told me," she muttered. "A couple times I wanted to call you and tell you that I had an opening for an appointment, if you were ready to take the next step, but I never could bring myself to make it happen." She looped her arms around his neck and smiled.

"I'm glad to hear that you thought about me," he whispered. "I was also worried that you would find somebody else to fill all your appointments with."

"That's what I do," she stated. "I work with people. Some cases are really bad. Some aren't, and some are incredibly rewarding because I may become too attached to the people I work with."

"Ah," he muttered, with a smile, "and I didn't want to be one of the people you became too attached to on a strictly work level."

"You've got that whole *work level* thing in your brain," she noted, tapping his temple. "You need to let it go."

"Why is that?"

"Because I don't get attached to people in my work. I care for them all. I work with them. I work hard with them," she explained, all with a smile, "and there are certainly benefits to working with them, but I don't want to get physical with them." She laughed. "And I don't even think about calling them to see if they want appointments."

"Did you ever call me?"

She nodded. "I did, but then I disconnected because you didn't answer right away. I took it as a sign I needed to *not* do it," she muttered. "But then I ran into you anyway, and here we are."

He smiled and kissed her softly. "Good." Her yawn caught him off guard, and he laughed. "You, my dear, need to get some sleep."

"I slept on the road, so why am I still tired?"

"Because neither one of us got any quality sleep at Rick's place."

"Right." She groaned. "So how about we pick this up later? We can both grab some sleep now, and then we'll talk—and eat—later."

"Sounds like a good idea to me," he murmured.

She grabbed her bag and said, "Come on upstairs." She

led the way to the second floor of her modest two-bedroom home. "This is a fairly new place for me."

"Is it? It's quite nice."

She showed him the spare room. "I'll go get a shower, then I'll crawl into bed."

"Good, and if you wake up in the night terrified ..."

"I know where you are," she said, with a big smile. "Let's hope I don't. The last thing I want is nightmares." She kissed him ever-so-gently on the lips and walked away. "Good night. We'll talk in the morning." And, with that, she disappeared into her room, and, as she closed the door, she caught herself grinning. Like a fool, she was head over heels with love and excitement, and yet she'd sent him to his room, alone. "Idiot," she muttered.

Then again she wasn't so sure. She didn't want to take things too crazy fast. Yet she had no intention of letting him go, not ever.

ONCE IN HIS room, Walton phoned Badger. He winced when he heard the sleepy voice on the other end. "Sorry, I didn't check the time."

"That's all right," Badger replied, as if trying to wake up in a hurry. "What's up?"

Walton quickly brought him up-to-date on what was happening with the car accidents on the highway, causing two more deaths.

"Jesus Christ, seriously?"

"Yeah, seriously." At a *woof* beside him, Walton looked down at the War Dog and smiled. "On the other hand, I do have Brutus here, and he's been a godsend on this trip."

"I'm glad something good worked out," Badger noted. "Everything else on that trip has been a nightmare."

"It is, and it won't end anytime soon."

"What do you mean?" Badger was never one to be slow on the uptake, and it was pretty obvious that he sensed something was wrong too.

"I don't have any justification for what I'm feeling. I don't have any reason for the suspicions that I have," Walton began.

"Ah, give me the rundown on what the hell you think is happening or about to happen."

Walton began, "I know it sounds ludicrous, but you found that George had a twin brother. I think the brother is up here."

"Yeah, and what about him?"

"I think he's the one behind it all."

"He does have a military record, and he certainly could be out there, living off the land quite easily," Badger agreed cautiously, "but what would his motivation be for killing all these people?"

"I'm not sure I have an answer for you on that one yet," Walton replied, staring out at nothing. "What I do know is that I don't think this is over. I feel as if he's still on a rampage."

"Did he see you?"

Walton hesitated. "I'm not sure, but he might very well have seen the War Dog, so it's possible he could have seen me all the same."

"Do you think George was telling him what was going on?"

"I think so, and, between the two of them, they managed to shoot Chad without anybody technically being on the scene."

"So, the twin brother came up in another vehicle, stayed hidden, and took care of Chad, and then, on the way home, takes out his own brother?"

"That was my impression, yes."

"So … that's a shitty deal," Badger noted. "The thing is, we're speculating. We don't even have a motive identified for any of this."

"I know. I don't have anything to even suggest that is what happened," Walton admitted. "All I can tell you is, when I was in the woods out by the lodge, I swear to God that I saw somebody who didn't want to be seen."

Silence came on the other end, while Badger thought about it. "I'll do a deeper investigation into the twins' backgrounds. We didn't even check out any of these guys ourselves because they weren't part of our original mission."

"I know, and, for that, I am sorry."

Badger snorted. "Every one of you guys who goes out looking for a War Dog ends up finding all kinds of other trouble."

"Not intentionally, though," Walton noted, with a sigh. "Still, when you send one of us out, and we find trouble, not even one of us will turn around and walk away."

"Nope, we don't do that shit. I'll get back to you in a little bit."

"Okay."

With that, Walton disconnected, then pulled out a notebook and sat here for a long moment, wondering what he was supposed to do. Then, with another thought—and pissed that it took him this long to think about it—he sent Badger a text, asking about Darren's location. He got a response back quickly.

Give us a minute.

Somebody would have to track down where Darren had gone. Had he flown all the way back home again, or was he stuck in town back there where the car went over into the ravine? Not sure what to do, Walton got up and paced. He stopped when he realized that Brutus was pacing with him. He chuckled, then bent down and grabbed the big guy around the rough of the neck and gave him a hug. "Just because I'm trying to work out some stress doesn't mean you need to as well, buddy." As he continued pacing, the dog kept pacing with him.

He sighed. "No way I'm letting you go. You know that, right?"

A *woof* came right back at him, and he smiled. "I want to believe that you knew what I just said, but, even if you don't, we'll still make one hell of a team."

Another *woof* came, and Walton continued to pace with Brutus. When his phone buzzed, it was a text message with the address of a hotel close by. Darren was staying there overnight, set to fly out tomorrow morning. As Walton read the message, his mind asked a question. *Would Darren still be alive by morning?* Walton realized that was the missing piece. It would take a little bit to get to the bottom of this, but Darren held the key. He was the last one alive, the only one who could provide some answers.

With that, Walton grabbed the lead and, motioning for Brutus, snuck downstairs. He slipped outside, jumped into his vehicle, and headed to the hotel. Making his way up to Darren's room, he knocked on the door.

A man answered from the other side, his voice trembling, "Who is it?"

"Hey, Darren. It's Walton, and I've got Brutus with

me." The bolt slid, and the door opened enough for Walton to see Darren, staring at him.

"What the hell are you doing here?" he asked Walton.

"I think we need to talk."

"No, no, no, I don't want to talk. I don't want to do anything but go home and try to forget this godforsaken weekend."

"What I'm trying to do is keep you alive."

Darren paled visibly, as he stared at him in shock. "What do you mean? What the fucking hell do you mean? Why would you suggest that?" he cried out.

"You know exactly what I mean," Walton said. "Somebody has been systematically killing off your entire group, and you're the only one with answers, and, if you don't give us answers now, … soon it'll be way too late because somebody will get to you too. Then nobody will ever know why it all happened."

"Don't say that," he snapped, shaking in his boots.

"Then come clean and tell me what the hell happened to Rudy."

He looked at him and repeated, "Rudy?"

"Yeah, Rudy. That's where it all started, wasn't it?"

His shoulders sagged, and he whispered, "No, it started earlier. Rudy … was just the worst of us."

"Oh, now that's interesting," Walton replied. "Do you want to fill in the rest of this for me?"

"Will you tell the cops?"

"Don't you think someone should?"

Darren stared at him, and then just wilted, literally right here in front of Walton. Darren opened the door enough for Walton and Brutus to walk inside. He looked at the dog nervously. "You went up there because of the dog, *huh*?"

"I did," Walton confirmed. "These War Dogs mean a lot to the men they served with."

"I can see that. He's also a hell of a lot better with you than he ever was with Chad." Darren threw himself down onto the small hotel couch and stared up at Walton. "What the hell do you want to know?"

"What happened to start all this?"

"What happened was, … we laughed at somebody," Darren began. "That's it. We laughed at him."

Walton stared at him for a long moment. "Depending on who you laughed at, and why, a man's pride is a pretty-big thing." He remembered the conversation he had just had with Chelsea about how a man's pride determined so many of his actions. "If you laughed at the wrong time, at the wrong person …"

"I know. I know," Darren wailed. "It was so stupid. It was really stupid, but it got out of hand, and Rudy wouldn't let it drop. He kept hassling him, making it out to be the joke of the year, but it was no longer funny."

"What was it about?"

"A woman, of course. Isn't it always about a woman?" Darren asked bitterly. "It was about a woman in a bar who Jacob was trying to pick up."

"Jacob, George's twin?" Walton asked.

Darren nodded. "She was pretty brutal with her rejection, and Jacob took it badly, but what we did to him afterward was pretty rough too, I guess. I wasn't even there for most of it, and I don't quite understand how it all got so bad, but apparently Rudy jumped in on it and started mocking Jacob for the rest of the night. Anybody could see that Jacob was getting angrier and angrier. Anybody could see a slowly burning buildup of fury grew inside Jacob, but

Rudy just wouldn't stop. We tried to cool it, but Rudy just kept at it and kept at it. The problem was, as soon as Rudy started it, then Chad picked it up too, and you saw how he could be."

"So, they were the ringleaders?"

"Pretty much. They were two peas in a pod. As soon as Rudy did it, Chad wanted in on it. So he would egg everybody else on, making it so that he was just part of the group, instead of the responsible ringleader. It was a bad night. I went home, got heavily drunk, and tried to forget about it, tried to forget about the guys. In case you hadn't noticed, they aren't exactly the nicest people."

"Were they all assholes that night?" Walton asked.

"I don't know if they were *all* assholes. I got fed up pretty quickly and left early. I just put them out of my mind for a long time. I used to get a lot of ribbing from them, but most of the time they left me alone. I guess, according to what they shared today, that they already knew back then that I was gay, but they never really bugged me about it."

"Maybe that's because they're also gay," Walton offered, with a note of humor.

Darren shook his head. "No, I don't think so. They couldn't ever acknowledge being gay themselves. That's why I'm surprised that they left me alone about it. Maybe they'd just had enough of bugging everybody or …"

"Or maybe they were getting ready to do something to you that was much worse."

Darren paled. "That would be more like it with these guys. They sure weren't acting normally. If Chad were still alive, and I announced I was gay to the group, Chad would have crucified me. He did crucify me, just individually, when blackmailing me to go on this stupid hunting trip. I have to admit that a part of me was pretty scared that I would end up … I don't want to say, *roasted alive*, but pretty-well *roasted alive* in a figurative sense," he muttered.

"And yet you still went."

"Yeah, because I was hoping Chad wouldn't tell anybody. Then I ended up telling them myself, and now they're all gone." Tears filled his eyes. "I don't even know what the hell's going on here," he whispered.

"So, I've got a couple questions for you. What did Jacob have to do with you guys?"

"We've all been friends for a very long time," Darren began, "and Jacob went into the military for quite a few years. When he got out, … he was different. His brother babied him, and we were like, *Dude, something is wrong with him. Leave him alone.*"

"He was ill?" Walton asked.

"To some degree. He seemed to get better over time, and he even seemed normal*ish* for quite a while. He didn't go off half-cocked quite so often, but he did end up getting quite ugly at times. During those times we were always very aware that he had a really short fuse, and I was always worried and never got in his way. I never did well with confrontations with anybody," he muttered, with a wave of his hands. "But Chad and Rudy? They just wouldn't lay off pushing Jacob's buttons. After this incident with the lady rejecting Jacob in the bar, I could tell it was bad news, but nobody would listen to me. I think … Hawk wasn't of the same ilk, but it's pretty-damn hard to walk away from the guys when they're in that kind of a mood."

"What kind of a mood exactly?" Walton steered him smoothly.

"They're ugly. They just don't stop. They keep badgering and badgering and badgering away at you," he shared. "Jacob didn't deserve it, and, as much as he seemed to be taking it, he wasn't really taking it well at all."

"Did anything happen to the woman?"

He frowned at him, startled. "You mean the woman who rejected Jacob?" He winced. "Yeah, something did happen, but it had nothing to do with Jacob."

"That depends on what happened," Walton stated.

"She got beat up in the bar's alleyway."

"You don't think it was Jacob?"

He shook his head. "He was with us the whole time."

"The *whole* time?" Walton asked. "Think about it. First, we have twins. Did you have your eye on George *and* Jacob for every minute afterward? It's pretty easy to slip out, go to the washroom, then catch some female also coming out of the washroom and beat the crap out of her for rejecting him."

He just stared at him and shook his head. "In that case … I don't know for sure," he admitted, "but, Jesus, I hope not. We should all have the right to reject whoever we want, and, if Jacob did beat up that woman, it would have been entirely because of her rejection of him at the pub that night. I wish I had never gone. God, I wish I'd never gone," he muttered, tears once again forming in his eyes. "Look at the hellish nightmare we're in now."

"That's what my question is about," Walton added. "Was it Jacob who got rejected, or was it George?"

Darren frowned. "Jacob. It was Jacob."

"Could you tell them apart?"

Darren grimaced, then shrugged. "Most of the time, yeah, and it wasn't really a problem. Particularly because Jacob had a short fuse, so that reaction was pretty easy to see.

You just had to prod the dragon to see one of them blow."

"Do you think that your friends did that?"

"Oh, yeah, they did it all the time. I know that sometimes they did it just because they couldn't tell them apart or because the two of them were trying to make it seem they were the other twin," Darren shared, "and that was a sick joke that they played on us, and we hated it."

"So, what are the chances that *Jacob* beat up that woman?"

"I would feel really terrible about it if he did," he stared at Walton. "That woman, … all she did was say no. The rest of it was basically the guys hassling Jacob."

"Okay, so this poor woman goes to a bar and ends up getting beaten up for rejecting one of the guys you're out with, and then Jacob still gets shit from Chad and Rudy? Jacob didn't tell Chad and Rudy what he did to the lady in the alleyway, yet he got his satisfaction, right? He got back at her for it."

"Sure, but it doesn't make any sense that he would turn around and do anything else. I mean, about the guys. She was the one who rejected him."

"But who are the ones who made fun of him?" Walton asked.

Darren stared at him. "But they were just making fun of him. Teasing him the way they always do."

"That's what I don't understand. Since when did teasing turn into something else, turn into a murderous rage? Because the teasing in this instance probably wasn't just teasing, was it?"

"It probably was hitting on a whole lot of other aspects that Jacob wouldn't or couldn't deal with," Darren admitted.

Walton stared at Darren, his mouth hanging open, maybe more fully aware now.

"Jacob was in sad shape already. He'd been having a lot of trouble since coming back from overseas. So, when he got rejected, the guys just threw him to the wolves, and it was rough, disgustingly rough. I couldn't believe all the things that they were saying, but Jacob just took it and took it and took it."

"And do you really think he *really* took it, *just* took it and took it?"

Darren looked at him and sighed. "No, I knew a fire was burning, a hatred was building inside. I just didn't know how it would look coming out. When Rudy died, and all of us were around, yet none of us were guilty, I didn't know what to think," he said. "Honestly, I thought Chad had done it."

"Why?"

"Because he's that kind of guy, yet I don't know that he had the gall to pull the trigger. He's one of those background kind of guys. He incites the riot, then fades into the background. He regularly gets all fired up, then doesn't follow through."

"Maybe that's a good thing."

"Oh, it's definitely a good thing. It's just not an easy thing. Jacob is still kind of … I don't know how to say it, but maybe not quite all there. That's letting him off the hook though, and I shouldn't do that." He gave a wave of his hand. "I don't know what his medical records say, but something is sad and outrageous about Jacob, and George used to always protect him. But that whole hunting trip thing? God, what a nightmare." He reached up a shaky hand. "Are you keeping the dog?" he asked abruptly.

Walton nodded. "Chad did have the balls to kill somebody," he shared, "because that old man died."

At that, tears once again came to Darren's eyes. He reached for a glass of water sitting nearby and drank nervously. "Jesus." He shook his head. "Just an old man sitting there with a dog?"

Walton nodded. "According to the neighbors, he and Chad got into an argument about something. Then it escalated and turned bad. Chad beat him up badly, then grabbed the dog from the backyard and ran. We got the news that the old man had died of his injuries shortly before we left the lodge."

"And, if Chad hadn't grabbed the dog, you probably wouldn't have him right now."

"I certainly would have started on a different path to find the War Dog," he stated, with a nod.

"And these guys might not have died."

"You think I'm to blame?" Walton asked, looking at him.

"No, no. I don't think you're to blame. I don't think that at all, man. I blame Chad. I'm just thinking about the series of events and how it all came about."

"Jacob is to blame too—or George, whoever was the bad twin that night. Plus, Chad added fuel to the fire, and the rest of you just jumped right into it with Chad and Rudy." Walton shook his head. "There is one thing here that I'm still trying to figure out. Why didn't Jacob come on the hunting trip with you?"

"Oh, that's easy. After all the teasing, Jacob wouldn't have anything to do with us anymore. He was pretty pissed, seriously pissed."

"So, knowing he's pretty pissed, do you really think Jacob didn't want to get back at you guys?"

"I'm sure he did, but I never saw him again, so I don't know."

"What if Rudy saw him beat up the woman?"

The color slowly drained from Darren's face as he realized what Walton was saying. "Oh my God."

"Is that something Jacob would do?" Walton asked him.

After just a moment of silence, he nodded. "Honest to God, yes. He's the kind of guy who has a slow-burning fury. He is methodical and would hang on to that retaliation, not doing something upfront but definitely over time. A surprise attack of revenge. Christ," he muttered, as he pinched the bridge of his nose, then dropped his hand and stared at Walton in shock, as if having a sudden realization. "You think Jacob killed the others?"

At that, Walton nodded. "Something is going on here that we're not quite sure of, but that would make sense, wouldn't it?"

"It would make sense, but that would also mean Jacob's coming after me." After saying that out loud, Darren paled further and started to shake. "Jesus Christ. Nobody will even know because everybody is already dead. And I'll soon be dead too."

At that, Walton kept his mouth closed as to which twin would show up, George or Jacob. "That would make sense, and that's one of the reasons I'm here."

"Why? You think he'll come here?" Jumping to his feet, Darren raced to the door, checking that it was locked.

"It is a consideration."

"No, no, no. I don't need this crap right now. Do you know how much therapy I've gone through in my life, just to try and *have* a life?"

"I'm sorry," Walton said, "but it does appear that you

hooked up with some pretty difficult friends."

"Ya think?" he quipped, tears still in his eyes. "High school was brutal for me."

"Got it," Walton noted. "What we have to do now is figure out just what the answer is here."

"I don't know that there can be an answer," Darren wailed. "How does anybody get an answer out of this shit?" He looked down at the dog. "Will you guys stay here?"

"Here? With you?" Walton asked.

"Yeah, I fly out in the morning. I just need you to stay long enough to get me onto that plane alive." Then he stopped, looked at him, and asked, "He wouldn't kill a whole planeload, would he?"

"I don't know. You tell me," Walton stated, eyeing him intently. "How much revenge are we looking at?"

Darren shook his head. "I don't know, but he's already killed everybody but me. I don't understand why it wasn't me first, as the easiest target, a *gay guy*."

"Maybe it was just a fluke. Were you all supposed to go to the lodge in one vehicle?"

"No, I was supposed to ride with Hawk, but, instead of me, George went." He stopped, then looked at him with a horrified expression. "Oh my God, oh my God, oh my God! Jacob didn't intend for his brother to die, did he?" He stared at Walton in shock. "Please tell me that's not what happened. Please don't tell me that, by changing places at the last minute, that I lived and his brother died. Now Jacob's ... Oh my God, he'll really be on the rampage now."

"I don't know," Walton admitted. "I'm a little late to this party you guys concocted, so it's a little hard for me to know the nuances quite the same as you."

"Maybe you've come to the party at just the right time. I

don't know what the hell is going on, but I feel as if I need police protection."

Walton shook his head. "Small town, just on the edge of nowhere," he pointed out. "You know perfectly well there won't be much in the way of police protection."

"No, there isn't, is there? Jesus Christ, what the hell have I done?"

"Presumably you came with your friends to share a hunting trip."

"I can't even kill anything," he shared, staring at him. "I would never shoot an animal. It was just another joke, another reason why they all wanted me to come, … so that I would suffer."

"You need to get new friends."

He gave a hysterical laugh. "Christ, maybe I'll just avoid the whole *friends* thing from now on." He looked around, almost in panic. "I don't even know where I can go. What can I do to avoid Jacob? How do I stop him?"

"First off, you don't do anything in a panic because, for one thing, we have to figure out where he is and how he could find you."

"I registered here under my own name," he cried out. "I wasn't even thinking that I needed to hide. Why would I? And, even if I did want to hide"—he shook his head—"I'm not good at that shit, but that's what Jacob does."

"What he *does*?" Walton repeated.

"Yes, it is exactly what he does," Darren confirmed. "That's the stuff he used to do in the military. Apparently he was really good at it."

Which wasn't good news as far as the current situation was concerned, but it wasn't any surprise to Walton. The military was very big on training.

At that came a sudden knock at the door. Darren let out a squeak and jumped to his feet. Looking over at Walton, he whispered, "What should I do?"

He thought about it and whispered back, "You can answer it."

"No way," he muttered, "no fucking way."

"How will you know who it is, if you won't even ask? Even if you don't, you'll spend the rest of your life looking behind you."

Just then somebody at the door called out, "Darren, let me in for Christ's sake. It's George."

Darren stared at Walton in shock.

"Just open the door, will you?" George asked again.

"I'm exhausted. I'm so fed up, and I'm tired, and I'm heartsick. Do you know they're all dead?" Darren cried out, and such pain filled his tone. "I mean, they're *dead*, dead."

"I know," George replied, his tone somber. "Come on, man. Open up the fucking door, and let me in."

Walton grabbed Brutus and hid behind the door, gesturing for Darren to open the door.

Darren frowned, not sure what he should, yet hesitant to see his friend, even if he was in need. Still, Darren walked to the door. "Are you unarmed?" he asked.

"What do you mean, am I unarmed? Of course I'm unarmed. Jesus Christ, did that K9 guy get to you? It's not as if I have anything to shoot you for. Isn't it enough that everybody's dead? Isn't it enough that all of us have suffered already?"

"It is for me," Darren admitted, and the relief in his tone was almost overwhelming. He popped open the door and then stepped back. "Come on in. You look like shit."

"Gee, thanks." He stepped in, and, before Darren had a

chance to even turn and walk back to the couch, George—if it was even George—jumped him, put him in a headlock, and dropped him to the floor, unconscious.

He pulled out a handgun, with a silencer on it.

Seeing that, Walton, already in the process of lunging, gave a silent command to Brutus. The War Dog jumped up, grabbed the other man by the gun hand, and brought him down with the force of his weight on top of the unconscious Darren. Walton jumped in, grabbing the gunman's arms, stopping him from reaching for the gun, which had gone spiraling across the room.

Walton gave him a hard right to the side of the head, momentarily stunning him. Walton grabbed his hands again, pulled them behind him, and pinned him to the floor. He looked around for something to tie the man's hands and saw the electrical cord on a lamp. Jerking on it, he shattered the lamp as he dragged it toward him. Quickly he tied up the man's wrists, even as he went to also tie up his legs. The cord thankfully was long enough that he could do a couple loops around both sets of limbs.

Walton hopped to his feet and, after a moment, got Brutus to release the wrist he still had in his mouth and then to stand guard. With that done, Walton searched for anything else he could additionally use to secure the prisoner with. He found another electrical cord on Darren's hair dryer in the bathroom.

With the gunman doubly secured and off to the side, Walton sent Badger a text, then bent down to see how Darren was.

Darren slowly opened his eyes, looked up at him, then whispered, "What happened?"

Walton motioned off to the side. "Your *friend* came to

visit," he said, with a sarcastic emphasis on *friend*.

Darren took one look, bolted to his feet with a shriek, and backed away. "My God, you were right."

"Yeah, unfortunately I was right. I'm just not sure how much I was right about though."

Darren frowned in confusion.

"Can you tell me if this is George, or is it really Jacob?"

He took a closer look but not very close, as if he were afraid the man would jump up and attack him again. "Jacob, I think."

"Pack up your stuff and get ready to leave. I'm not saying you'll get to leave, but the police are coming now."

"Right," he muttered, keeping a nervous eye on George or Jacob, whoever it was. Darren quickly packed up his stuff and set it by the door. "Jesus Christ," he muttered, "you have no idea how much I want to go home."

"Home is upcoming," Walton said, "and, with any luck, this will put an end to it."

"Put an end to what? Did he really kill everybody?"

Almost on cue, the other man spoke. "Kill who?" He sneered at Darren. "Are you asking about all those sniveling pieces of shit? Damn right, I killed them all. Did you think I would let that slide?"

Darren stared at him. "Why did you kill your own brother?"

After a moment he said, "I didn't mean to. *You* were supposed to be in that vehicle, but you changed places at the last minute. Why did you do that?"

"Damn right I did. Jesus Christ, you should know that Hawk is a madman on the highway, and I never want to ride with him."

"I was counting on him being a madman on the highway, and I knew that, once I cut that brake line, one of those nasty corners would send them off the road. I just didn't know which one it would be," he muttered. "What do you care? You got off. You survived, and you weren't supposed to."

"I'm sorry," he cried out, staring at him.

"Of course you're sorry. You're all sorry now. You think Rudy wasn't sorry when he realized what was happening? Do you think Chad wasn't sorry when he saw me?"

"But did he know it was you and not George?"

"I don't know whether he knew it was me or not," Jacob replied. "He might not have noticed right at the beginning, but he sure knew by the end."

"You were talking to him?"

"I was. Everybody thought they saw George, but it was me." Jacob sneered. "After I killed Chad, I disappeared pretty-damn fast, then told my brother where the body was. He was pissed at me, but he understood."

"What do you mean, he understood? How could he have understood?… You were killing all these people, our supposed friends."

"Yeah, killing all these people, people who were black-mailing *friends*, people who were pieces of shit."

"Did George expect you to kill all of us? Was that something George was okay with?" Darren asked, staring at Jacob, still nervous.

"I don't know if he was okay with all that, but I wouldn't stop until I knew everybody had paid for all the shit they put me through."

"Even me?" Darren asked sadly. "I didn't do anything to you."

At that, Jacob shrugged. "Maybe not," he conceded,

"but, in my mind, you're still associated with all of it. So, yeah, you too."

"So, you came here intending to kill me?" Darren sat down, pulled his knees up to his chest, and just rocked back and forth. "I don't think I'm ever traveling again."

"Yeah, you probably shouldn't," Jacob agreed. "You're really not built for it."

"Ya think? Yet your brother and all the rest of the *bros* had such fun making my life hell."

"In that case you should be happy they're all gone," Jacob stated, twisting his head to try and face Darren. Jacob's gaze landed on Brutus, and his lips curled. "What the hell? A fucking War Dog? How the hell did I leave the military and end up with a War Dog bringing me down?"

"Did you leave the military or were you dishonorably discharged?" Walton asked.

He twisted ever-so-slightly. "You …"

"So, you sure made Chad pay, didn't you?"

Jacob laughed. "I made sure they *all* paid. I guess it's fair enough that a War Dog got me because those were the best days of my life. After my injury, I got sidelined, and it's just not the same anymore. I was good at what I did," he declared passionately. "I mean, the accident should never have happened to me."

"I get what you must be feeling. Yet instead of taking it out on whatever caused the accident, here you are taking it out on your friends."

"The accident was *because* of my friends," he declared, "and partly because of the accident itself. I was home on leave, and we went out drinking. I forget who was driving, but we had run off the road and into a tree. We were all so drunk that none of us was badly hurt. Yet my head hit the dashboard, and I seemed to be different afterward. And that *joke's on you* attitude they had just hit me wrong," he explained, with another sneer. "I don't understand quite how it worked, but I can tell you that, from one minute to the next, … all I could think about was taking them down and making them pay for laughing at me, over that damn bitch."

"So, a payback plan was born. How did you do it?"

"After the car accident and my *failure to follow orders*, I was discharged. All of a sudden, I had all this free time available, and I needed something to turn my attention to. So I bided my time. I just waited, letting all that anger churn in my gut," he explained, with a smirk. "That's what I did. So, like it or not, it was worth every damn bit of waiting."

"I hope you feel that way after you spend the rest of your life in jail," Walton noted, "because that won't be any picnic for a guy like you."

"Maybe not," he agreed, "but those assholes in jail? They won't fucking touch me either. I'll just kill them. I really don't care. At this stage in my life, I would just as soon die by suicide or suicide by cop."

"You won't have that opportunity right now," Walton murmured. "My job is to hand you over. After that, it's up to you."

He stared at him. "Got it."

It was almost as if he made a plan at that very moment in time. Walton returned the stare. "Don't take anybody else with you, Jacob."

He shrugged. "Like I give a fuck."

Another knock came on the door just after that, and the cops arrived, and that chaos began. Walton stepped back and looked over at Darren. He was trembling still. "As soon as you're done here, get your ass to the airport and go home."

Darren looked at him and nodded. "As soon as I'm done with the police, I'm taking a cab, and I'm going home. I'll try and forget that I ever knew any of these people," he muttered, crying now.

Detective Hogan had arrived and was talking to the officers on the scene. He stepped closer to Walton and Darren, nodding at both of them in acknowledgment. "Don't forget," he told them both, "you may have to show up for a trial."

Darren swallowed several times and then nodded bravely. "I think I can do that."

"That's all good and dandy then."

Walton turned to Detective Hogan. "Good, in that case I'm leaving. You can catch me for a statement tomorrow." He handed him his contact information. "I'm taking the dog out of here. Way too many people got here very quickly, and I, for one, have had enough for now. So has Brutus."

Detective Hogan looked at the dog and nodded. "We'll catch up with you tomorrow."

With that, Walton and Brutus headed outside and back to Chelsea's place. As he walked in the door, she stood there, her arms wrapped around her chest, staring at him.

"Are you okay?" she murmured.

He gave her a small smile. "That's a better greeting than I expected it would be. I figured maybe I would get reamed out for leaving."

"No, I knew you were heading to Darren. Did you find him? Save him?"

He gave her a slow nod and smiled. "I did, and now it's over."

"Is it really?" She stared at him hopefully.

"Yes," he confirmed. As he walked her upstairs, he explained what happened. He answered her myriad of questions, while she sat down on the side of his bed and just stared at him. "Dear God, people can be the meanest of the mean."

"And yet you get a group of mean people together, and they turn into something even uglier," Walton noted.

"He didn't mean to kill his brother, *huh*?"

"No, he didn't, but he was also planning on ending either his brother's life afterward or his own. I don't think he even contemplated what his choices were back at that point in time."

"It still sucks," she muttered. "Poor Darren."

"Poor Darren, but believe me that Darren is damn lucky right now. He's on his way home, … probably to never ever leave it again. Although he has to face the trial. If this didn't scar him for life, that will."

"No, I'm sure he won't ever leave," she muttered, as she studied Walton. "What about you?"

"What about me? … I'm fine. I was thinking a shower and some sleep would be a good idea. I gave up on that earlier."

"You sure did," she muttered, staring at him.

"When did you realize I left?"

"Right away. I seem to have some insider cues, when it comes to you."

He grinned. "I kind of like that."

She laughed. "You do realize that just means, if you ever try to sneak around, you won't do it successfully."

"Wasn't really planning on doing it at all," he stated. "I just didn't want to get you into another dangerous situation."

She nodded. "Because of that I'm not pissed."

"That's a good thing," he said, with a bright smile. "I wasn't exactly sure how you would respond at the end of the day."

"I'm a big girl," she said, "and I understand that a whole lot in this world doesn't work out the way we want it to, even if we thought we could make it happen in whatever way."

He nodded in agreement.

"I am, however, very happy that you're home, safe and sound." She bent down and cuddled Brutus, who was stretched out on the carpet in front of her. "What about this guy?"

"I'm keeping him," he stated. She looked up in delight, and he nodded. "Detective Hogan even suggested that I might want to start a career helping law enforcement around here. They could use an asset like Brutus."

"Oh my, that would be excellent."

"It certainly would be putting his training and mine to good use, and that is a great thing." He pulled his T-shirt off over his head and then sat down on the side of the bed and pulled off his sock.

When he got up to take off his jeans, she stood up. "Do you need help with the leg?"

"Maybe, I'm pretty damn tired."

"Of course you are," she muttered. "You drove the whole way to the lodge and then back again and were supposed to go to sleep hours ago."

"I was trying to. It just didn't work out so well."

She didn't say anything. No recriminations, no telling him off, no scolding, no nothing. Whether that would come tomorrow or not, he didn't know, but, for now, it was a godsend. By the time she had his leg off and ointment working its way up his sore muscles, he sighed happily. "I need the prosthetic, but I also feel a certain freedom when not wearing it."

"Of course," she agreed. "It's one of those things that's a necessary tool, but it comes with its own challenges."

"Doesn't it though?" When he got up and hopped his way to the bathroom, she stood. "Do you need any help?"

"You can turn on the shower for me, if you want to."

She came in, fired up the shower, and turned around to see him, standing there completely nude. As he sat on the edge of the tub, he swung himself over inside the tub, then stood up.

She frowned. "It's not the kind of shower you're used to," she noted cautiously.

He shrugged. "No, but I can make do."

"We can make adjustments to it."

He looked at her in surprise and then shrugged. With a grin, he asked, "What is the shower in your bedroom like?"

"Damn, I never even thought of that. I should have just had you shower in there. The bathtub and the shower are separate."

"A standalone shower is easier for me to get in and out of," he agreed, with a nod. "That's all right. I can try it next time."

A few minutes later, after sending her off, saying he could handle this alone, he finished shampooing his hair, shut off everything, and sat down on the side of the bathtub to give his leg a break. He quickly dried off and then, using the wall, hopped his way back out into his bedroom. She was sitting cross-legged on his bed, wearing just a tiny little nightie.

She looked up and smiled. "I know you're tired."

"I am tired," he said, "but I don't think anybody is ever *that* tired."

She chuckled. "We can also just sleep."

"We could," he murmured, "but it's been a rough day and a very rough evening, and I would very much like to hold a warm, willing woman in my arms and let everything else in the world disappear for a while."

She immediately opened her arms. "Sounds good to me."

He made his way to the side of the bed and collapsed down. Laughing, she leaned over and kissed him gently. "If you're too tired, honestly, I'm totally okay to sleep. We do have time."

"We do have time," he murmured, as he nuzzled her cheek and neck. "But somehow I feel a sense of not *urgency* exactly, but"—he stared off in the distance briefly—"maybe just a sense of completion."

"Oh, I like that too." She slipped her nightie over her head and settled her warm body against his, still hot and slightly damp. She rubbed her chest across his and whispered, "There is definitely something freeing about being here like this."

"I know," he muttered, "and it would have been nice if we could have shared this at your brother's lodge. It was a magical place."

"He really wants us to return sometime," she said, with a grin. "I just don't want to go back alone."

"Nope, but we can go back together." He wrapped his arms around her and pivoted, so she was beneath him.

"Wow, you might not have a leg," she muttered, "but it doesn't seem to hold you back."

"I'm not sure that *not* having a leg should have anything

to do with it," he noted, with a smile. "It's a leg. I still have another one." He lifted himself up on his arms. "Besides, it'll be a long, cold day in hell if I don't make the absolute most of every moment I have with you in my arms."

She stared up at him, tears in her eyes, and whispered, "Me too."

CHAPTER 13

CHELSEA WRAPPED HER arms around Walton, her fingers sliding through his curls and yet not curls. They were more waves, yet here and there were the odd really tight curls. She smiled in joy at the discovery, as she now stroked the huge muscles across his shoulders and down his back. "You may have wanted to come to me in a better shape," she shared, "but honestly, you were in damn-good shape to begin with, and now you're in better shape than ever."

"Good, that was the plan."

She chuckled. "Job well done."

He smiled, leaned over, kissed her, and she very quickly lost herself in the gentle movement of his lips, the gentle probing of his tongue, as the heat slowly began to build and started to curl her toes. She wrapped her thighs around his hips, pulling him closer into position, her legs sliding down to the edge of his stump and then falling to the second leg below.

He lifted his head. "Does it bother you?"

"No, of course it doesn't bother me," she said, tapping his nose. "I would think that would be a question you wouldn't need to ask me, of all people."

He nuzzled her cheek and nodded. "Still looking for reassurance, I guess."

It startled her, and yet it shouldn't have because, no matter how strong and invincible we all appear to be, everybody had their vulnerabilities, and, for him, this was obviously one of them. "I didn't care about it in the beginning, and I don't care about it now," she declared. "You're not defined by the body part missing in your world."

Then she pulled him down and gave him a searing kiss, trying to convince him of the truth of her words. And it seemed to have worked because he suddenly moaned and seared her with an absolutely intensifying electric kiss that tingled her toes, as she tightened her thighs hard around him. She was still in a haze when he lifted his head, and she whispered, "What the hell was that?"

"That was an onslaught of love," he murmured, as he kissed her again and again and again, sliding his way down her body to kiss every inch of her, as he slid right to her toes, taking her big toe and nibbling it.

She burst out laughing, then tried to pull her feet away because of the tickling. "You can't do that," she gasped. "That's just not fair."

"Oh, don't I know it," he muttered. "All is fair in love and war."

"Nope, nope, nope."

Laughing he pulled away and slid all the way back up her body, and this time he opened her thighs wide, and he slid right into position. "Will this tickle too?" he asked.

"God, I hope not," she whispered, "but I sure as hell know it'll feel good."

When he slid deep inside to find her warm and welcoming center, she sighed, happily shifting beneath him to adjust to him. He looked at her with an eyebrow raised, and she smiled. "I'm fine. I'm fine at the moment, but, if you make me wait too much longer, I won't be."

He chuckled and started to move.

She wrapped her arms around him, enjoying the ride and loving the feeling of having him here where she had wanted him for so long—loving their ability to share, their ability to communicate, and just to be themselves with each other. And then she couldn't think at all, as the two became one. He took the pace faster and faster and drove her over the edge. She dimly heard him come, before he collapsed into her arms.

Shifting to the side, he pulled her up against his chest and whispered, "Now we can sleep."

Smiling, she drifted off and slept deeply.

When she woke the next morning, she was a little on the sore side, having woken up several times in the night, made love, then gone back to sleep again. This time she rolled over, and he was sitting up, leaning against the headboard, talking softly on the phone.

He looked at her with a smile and stroked the hair off her face, then continued with his call. "Yeah, I'll be here. I'd like to just spend some time getting to know the dog, seeing what his capabilities are, but, yeah, I do want to keep him."

She remembered him mentioning something about maybe working with the police, and she presumed Badger was on the other end. She was delighted at the idea.

When Walton got off the phone, he slid down and pulled her into his arms. "Good morning, gorgeous."

She chuckled in delight. "That's not a bad way to wake up."

"Of course it's not a bad way to wake up," he agreed, nuzzling her once again. "But I've got to tell you, our new pet is definitely looking to go out."

Brutus. Almost as if he understood they were talking

about him, Brutus made a sudden leap and ended up on the bed, on top of them.

She burst out laughing. "So, is this my life from now on?" she asked in a teasing tone.

"It could be, if you want it to be."

"I want it to be," she declared instantly, looking at him with a bright smile. "I would love it to be like this." She leaned over. "But you take a little longer to get dressed, so up and at 'em, buddy. You have a dog to look after."

"What?" he protested, laughing. "You'll let me go out there, all alone in that cold morning air, and face the world without you?"

"Oh, does that mean you want me to come along?"

"Of course I do. Honestly, given a choice, … I want you at my side for the rest of my life."

She held out her hand and, with a big smile, said, "Deal."

BADGER PUT DOWN his phone and looked at Kat. "That turned out better than expected."

"Yeah, but what the hell's wrong with our world, when they go after a dog and end up with some other crazy scenario that none of us could even see coming?"

"I think that's just life," he said, with a nod. "However, you're right. We just barely get things straightened up, and something else goes haywire. You don't have another case now, right?"

"Not so sure about that. … We still have Timber to deal with."

"Sure, still Timber to deal with, but he will always be somebody we're dealing with," he pointed out. "He's not set up, but I know he's getting closer."

She nodded. "So there just might be something else." Then she pulled out two file folders from among her stack.

"More?"

"I did tell them that we will be enlisting Timber's help down the road with further cases, but they didn't think there should be any more. They've instituted some new changes."

Badger added, "Yet one or two more War Dogs might still be caught up in the old system though."

"But the new changes should help a lot."

"Do we believe them when they say that?" he teased,

with an eye roll. "Besides, you seem to be handling this job just fine."

"Sure, but that doesn't mean I'm ideally suited for this type of work, especially when my development of new prosthetics is really taking off, for humans and animals."

"That's true enough too," Badger agreed, "so where is this first case starting from?"

"Michigan."

"What's going on there?"

"A family with a paralyzed boy adopted the War Dog, but then his parents were killed in a car accident. Unfortunately, the boy was put into foster care because he had no relatives ready to step up and take him, and the dog has since disappeared."

"Oh, good Lord," Badger muttered, shaking his head. "That's not good. Every boy needs a dog, and it sounds as if these two need each other."

"If it's the boy's dog, the loss would be very hard on both the boy and the dog," she agreed, "and our job is to find the dog."

"And to sort out whether the boy can get the dog back."

"That can only happen if anybody is willing to take both him and the War Dog," she noted. "Unfortunately, when an entire family gets wiped out like that, the odds aren't great to place both, particularly when they each have disabilities."

Badger shook his head at that. "Tell me that you have somebody in Michigan."

"No, I sure don't." She hesitated.

"But?"

"I might know somebody, but I haven't talked to him for a long time."

"What's his name?"

"Shelton."

He frowned at her. "Cage Shelton?"

"Yeah."

"Why would you think he would be a good fit for this job?" he asked curiously.

She shrugged. "I'll say *instincts*, but also I know that he was raised with dogs. He's ex-military of course," she added, "but, more than that, his younger brother was also in a wheelchair."

Badger gazed at his wife, and a slow smile dawned on his face. "Not the typical matchmaking of a couple, yet I can see the similarities between our case and Cage's life. Plus, you want to help everyone. Just right up your alley, isn't it?"

She shrugged. "Breaks my heart to think that the War Dog bonded to a boy who needed him desperately, and now the boy has lost not only his family but also his dog."

"Yeah, that's not fair, is it? So, what is it you expect Cage to do?" he asked, now curious.

She gave him a bright smile. "Everything, absolutely everything."

"At this point I expect miracles from every one of our guys," Badger declared.

She laughed. "It doesn't hurt to expect miracles. That doesn't mean they always happen, but, in this case, … I've got a feeling."

This concludes Book 26 of The K9 Files: Walton.
Read about Cage: The K9 Files, Book 27

The K9 Files: Cage (Book #27)

Welcome to the all new K9 Files series reconnecting readers with the unforgettable men from SEALs of Steel in a new series of action packed, page turning romantic suspense that fans have come to expect from USA TODAY Bestselling author Dale Mayer. Pssst… you'll meet other favorite characters from SEALs of Honor and Heroes for Hire too!

Finding a missing K9 dog is a great way to give back to both the people and the animals who have helped Cage over the years. He didn't expect his actions to help someone else—maybe even himself. Yet that's the likely outcome when he realizes the dog belongs to a little boy who suffers from spina bifida and who lost his parents in a car accident. Now Cage must save a little boy and his dog, who need each other more than ever.

Risa never should have split from Cage years ago, and seeing the man he is now just accents all she has lost. Even harder is the realization that time did not change anything between them. He is still the one for her.

Yet getting to a happy future looks less and less likely, as the two of them realize something sinister underlies this whole mess, and someone doesn't want them to survive …

Find Book 27 here!
To find out more visit Dale Mayer's website.
https://geni.us/DMSCage

Author's Note

Thank you for reading Walton: The K9 Files, Book 25! If you enjoyed the book, please take a moment and leave a short review.

Dear reader,

I love to hear from readers, and you can contact me at my website: www.dalemayer.com or at my Facebook author page. To be informed of new releases and special offers, sign up for my newsletter or follow me on BookBub. And if you are interested in joining Dale Mayer's Reader Group, here is the Facebook sign up page.
http://geni.us/DaleMayerFBGroup

Cheers,
Dale Mayer

About the Author

Dale Mayer is a *USA Today* best-selling author, best known for her SEALs military romances, her Psychic Visions series, and her Lovely Lethal Garden cozy series. Her contemporary romances are raw and full of passion and emotion (Broken But … Mending, Hathaway House series). Her thrillers will keep you guessing (Kate Morgan, By Death series), and her romantic comedies will keep you giggling (*It's a Dog's Life*, a stand-alone novella; and the Broken Protocols series, starring Charming Marvin, the cat).

Dale honors the stories that come to her—and some of them are crazy, break all the rules and cross multiple genres!

To go with her fiction, she also writes nonfiction in many different fields, with books available on résumé writing, companion gardening, and the US mortgage system. All her books are available in print and ebook format.

Connect with Dale Mayer Online

Dale's Website – www.dalemayer.com

Twitter – @DaleMayer

Facebook Page – geni.us/DaleMayerFBFanPage

Facebook Group – geni.us/DaleMayerFBGroup

BookBub – geni.us/DaleMayerBookbub

Instagram – geni.us/DaleMayerInstagram

Goodreads – geni.us/DaleMayerGoodreads

Newsletter – geni.us/DaleNews